"Krissy wanted you to raise him, child. Raise him like he was your own," Grandpa said.

Paige's mouth opened. Not a sound came out. She'd been named Bryan's *guardian?*

Why in the world—

She'd always assumed Grandpa would be there if anything—

She couldn't possibly—

Looking to the other end of the table, she realized Jay and Bryan were as shocked as she was. Mouths gaped open. Both of them struck dumb.

As if the words Grandpa had spoken had finally registered, Bryan's eyes widened. His face turned red. He leaped to his feet.

"I don't want her to be my guardian!" he screamed. "I want my mom!" Knocking over his chair, Bryan raced from the room and out the back door.

Stunned, Paige sent up a heartfelt prayer. *Please, Lord, what am I supposed to do now?*

Books by Charlotte Carter

Love Inspired

Montana Hearts
Big Sky Reunion
Big Sky Family
Montana Love Letter
Home to Montana
Montana Wrangler

CHARLOTTE CARTER

A multipublished author of more than fifty romances, cozy mysteries and inspirational titles, Charlotte Carter lives in Southern California with her husband of forty-nine years and their cat, Mittens. They have two married daughters and five grandchildren. When she's not writing, Charlotte does a little stand-up comedy, "G-Rated Humor for Grown-ups," and teaches workshops on the craft of writing.

Montana Wrangler
Charlotte Carter

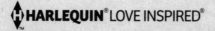

HARLEQUIN® LOVE INSPIRED®

Recycling programs
for this product may
not exist in your area.

 ™ LOVE INSPIRED BOOKS

ISBN-13: 978-0-373-81705-4

MONTANA WRANGLER

Copyright © 2013 by Charlotte Lobb

This is a work of fiction. Names, characters, places and incidents are
either the product of the author's imagination or are used fictitiously, and
any resemblance to actual persons, living or dead, business establishments,
events or locales is entirely coincidental.

This edition published by arrangement with Love Inspired Books.

® and TM are trademarks of Love Inspired Books, used under license.
Trademarks indicated with ® are registered in the United States Patent
and Trademark Office, the Canadian Trade Marks Office and in other
countries.

www.LoveInspiredBooks.com

Printed in U.S.A.

Trust in the Lord with all your heart and lean not on your own understanding; in all your ways acknowledge Him and He will make your paths straight.
—*Proverbs 3:5–6*

I want to express my appreciation
to the readers on the Harlequin Forums
who helped me to "grow" Bear Lake, Montana, with
their creative ideas: Loves 2 Read Romance, who
suggested Loves 2 Read Romance Bookshop
& Bakery, and Valri, who envisioned the
chatty postmistress in town.

Special thanks to my editor, Emily Rodmell,
who makes me write better books.

Chapter One

Tears blurred Paige Barclay's vision as she stood on the wide plank porch of her grandpa Henry's house in the high country of western Montana not far from Glacier National Park.

She hadn't cried at her sister's funeral that morning. Their mother had always said crying was a waste of time and energy. Now, alone with her thoughts and her sense of guilt and regret, Paige's tears were hard to hold back.

Paige eyed the horses shifting around in the nearby corral—her grandfather's stable of horses used in his Bear Lake Outfitters operation. Their tails flashed as they flicked flies away. They stomped their feet. Occasionally they snorted or tossed their heads from side to side as though warning Paige to keep her distance.

Even from several hundred feet, she caught the

earthy animal scent, which almost overwhelmed the more pleasant perfume of pine trees.

She wrinkled her nose. Did everyone in Montana have to own a horse?

She'd been terrified of horses almost as long as she could remember. Their size. Their big teeth. And that she'd been dumped from the saddle when she was five years old. A memory she couldn't forget and one that still gave her nightmares. A broken leg. Pain. Surgery that left a scar she could still see.

Her mother upset and angry because she had to stay home to take care of Paige instead of working at the family's hardware store.

Everything about Bear Lake and the outfitting business was entirely different from Paige's life and her career in Seattle. In the same way, Paige and her younger sister Krissy had had little in common.

Krissy had loved horses, loved riding them, the faster the better. Four days ago, not far from here, riding a horse too fast, jumping the horse too far, had killed Krissy.

Growing up, everyone had said Krissy was the pretty sister. The fun-loving sister. Paige was the good sister. The plain sister.

Being pretty hadn't done Krissy much good.

"My sister shouldn't have died so young," she said aloud, as though accusing the horses in the corral.

"If she hadn't been riding so recklessly," a smooth

baritone voice announced, "Krissy wouldn't have died, and I wouldn't have had to put a good horse down."

Thinking that she'd been alone, she started. Turning, she discovered Jay Red Elk had walked silently up onto the porch and was now looming over her. Considering she was a good five foot seven or eight, depending on which pair of high heels she wore, that was quite a feat.

Of course, her grandfather's wrangler and trail guide stood well over six feet. His unreadable expression and more than a hint of his Blackfoot heritage in his chiseled cheekbones made him an intimidating figure. Not that she had any intention of backing down to him.

She realized during her occasional visits to Montana in the past few years she hadn't paid much attention to Jay and had purposefully kept her distance from him and his horses. Mostly his horses, she realized.

Now she took a closer look at his hard, potently masculine physique, his closed expression and felt a shiver of awareness scurry down her spine.

"Krissy was reckless from the day she was born," Paige admitted, her throat tight with the tears she hadn't shed. The wildness and rebellion ingrained in Krissy's personality had culminated in her pregnancy at age fifteen. Their parents had sent her here to live with their grandparents and to raise her son,

Bryan. Apparently the change of scenery hadn't tamed her spirit.

Jay rested his lean hips on the rustic porch railing and folded his arms across his broad chest. "She didn't respect her horse or the land that is God's gift to us. Perhaps if she had lived longer, she might have grown more wise."

Shaking her head, Paige wasn't at all sure age would have changed her sister. She was surprised, however, to hear the depth of caring in Jay's voice. Perhaps living so close to the land, guiding others through the nearby wilderness areas, had given him a respect for both his horses and the rest of the Lord's creations. She could admire that in a man.

"There were quite a few people at the funeral this morning. She must have had a lot of friends." Paige, who often found herself in her sister's shadow, had envied Krissy her popularity, but not the arguments and fights she perpetually had with their parents. Those battles had sent Paige fleeing to the safety of her room to hide behind a closed door.

"Bear Lake's a small town," Jay said. "Friendly, for the most part. Everyone knew Krissy. Some more than others."

She winced, suspecting those who knew Krissy the best were men eager to take advantage of her. The few relationships Krissy had talked about during Paige's infrequent visits had seemed like disasters in the making.

Despite herself, Paige wondered what the relationship had been between Jay and her sister. Had he succumbed to Krissy's charms? Not that it was any of her concern.

"I would have thought you and Krissy would have had a lot in common." Two attractive people. Horse lovers. How could they not have found themselves drawn to each other?

She felt his eyes, shadowed beneath the brim of his hat, surveying her. "Krissy wasn't my type."

No? What was his type, she wondered.

"Bryan seems pretty quiet for a kid," she said, intentionally shifting her thoughts away from Krissy. Although Paige always sent Bryan birthday and Christmas gifts, she hadn't spent too much time one-on-one with him. In recent years during her short visits, he much preferred to be outside with the horses than visiting with Aunt Paige. Now she wished she'd tried harder to get to know him. "How do you think he's taking his mom's death?"

"Like any twelve-year-old, I guess. He loved his mother." Pushing away from the railing, he shoved his fingertips in the hip pockets of his new jeans and stood looking past Paige toward the corral. Instead of his usual dusty work clothes, he'd worn a turquoise western-cut shirt with a silver bolo tie and a dressy black Stetson to the funeral service at the community church in town. He hadn't changed yet. He thumbed his hat back to a rakish angle. "He's confused. Missing her, I suppose. He spends most of his time either at school or with the horses anyway. He's getting to be quite a good trail hand."

She shuddered at the thought of her young nephew spending so much of his time on a horse. Raised in Lewiston, in a small town in Montana prairie country, Paige was now a full-fledged city girl.

"I hope Grandpa Henry doesn't let Bryan go riding off by himself," she said.

Shifting his attention back to her, Jay's startling blue-green eyes widened and his dark brows lifted. "Why not?"

"Well, because he could get lost. Or hurt." That seemed perfectly obvious to her. This was wilderness country.

"If he got lost, he'd follow his own tracks back to where he started just like I've taught him." Jay shrugged. "As for getting hurt, that can happen to any kid, even ones who live in a big city like Seattle. If you ask me, a kid's better off living here than most any other place I could think of."

She disagreed, and certainly didn't care for his attitude about the city she now called home. After all, Seattle had wonderful parks and schools, topnotch cultural activities and every sporting event imaginable.

She lifted her chin. "I'm going to check on Grandpa. See if I can fix him something to eat." The ladies of the church had provided a buffet lunch following the funeral service even though they hadn't known Krissy well. But she'd noticed Grandpa had barely touched any of the salads or casseroles. "If you could round up Bryan, I'll fix him something, too. Of course, you're welcome to join us."

One corner of his firm lips lifted into an imitation of a smile. "Thanks. I'll come in later."

Jay waited a moment after Paige went inside, then stepped off the porch. He strolled to the bunkhouse where he had his private quarters.

Whenever Paige had shown up at Bear Lake, she'd made no secret of her feelings about Henry's outfitting business. Or her sister's behavior. Granted, she'd been polite, and she'd tried to make friends with Bryan. But a career woman like Paige, who had some hotsy-totsy corporate job with a big hotel chain, had no clue what little boys liked to do.

She'd kept her distance from Jay. Unlike Krissy, who had fallen all over herself trying to seduce him with her bubbly personality and seductive body. He'd known right off that Krissy wasn't a woman interested in a long-term commitment. Once he'd made it clear that he was having none of it, she had moved on to someone more accommodating.

In the process, she often left Bryan's parenting needs to Henry and his late wife, Lisbeth. Over time, Jay had simply picked up some of the slack with Bryan—a good kid who needed a bit of encouragement and guidance.

Oddly, he'd always found Paige more physically appealing than Krissy. Paige seemed more natural than her younger sister, for all that she'd traded a small town for a big city. Instead of bleaching her hair nearly white like Krissy, she'd left it the color she'd been born with, a shade that reminded him of the sleek strands of a palomino's mane. A straight nose and a cute little chin gave her an innocent look. Not as curvaceous as her sister, Paige was a more petite package, yet still feminine.

Not that he ever intended to act on his attraction to Paige. Like always, she'd be gone in a few days. Back to the crowds, traffic congestion and wealthy guests who stayed at her hotel. He wouldn't even try to compete with that.

Jay's apartment consisted of a living room, one bedroom, a bath with a claw-foot tub and a kitchen that was barely big enough to turn around in. Most of the time he ate in the big house with the family, so about all he did in his kitchen was brew coffee, which he drank black and potent.

For an emergency, he kept a jar of peanut butter on hand and some bread in the freezer.

His mother, who lived in Browning on the east side of the Rocky Mountains, kept him well supplied with photos of his nieces and nephews, which he propped on the end table next to the broken-down couch.

A photograph of his wife, Annie, took center stage among the other pictures. Annie had died trying to give birth to their stillborn son nearly six years ago. Annie had been everything a man could want—smart, funny, with dark eyes that sparkled when she smiled, and she rode a horse like she'd been born in the saddle.

Ignoring the familiar tightness in his chest, he went into the bedroom to change into a pair of well-worn jeans, scuffed boots and a comfortable shirt. Although he had a local kid who took care of the horses and was learning to be a trail guide, Jay never took that for granted. The animals were his responsibility.

Paige found her grandfather sitting in his recliner in the living room staring off into space. At eighty-five, he was still lean, his arms striped with ropy muscles, but his hair had thinned, revealing brown age spots the gray strands barely covered. From years in the sun, his face had taken on the look of a topographical map crisscrossed by rivers and canyons.

The room itself was familiar to Paige: the knotty-pine paneling, overstuffed furniture, photographs of Bear Lake on the wall and the upright piano she used to play with Grandma Lisbeth when her family came to visit. Those visits had been rare, her father reluctant to close the hardware store for even a few days.

No wonder she had dreamed of trips abroad, places far from Lewiston and the endless Montana prairie.

"Grandpa, are you hungry? I can fix you something to eat."

Blinking, he turned his watery blue eyes toward her. "I'm going to miss that girl."

"I know." Paige sat on the arm of the couch next to him and took his hand, his fingers gnarled and callused from hard work. Given his age, she wondered if he'd be up to raising Bryan on his own now without Krissy around to help out. Or perhaps he'd been doing exactly that since Grandma Lisbeth passed on.

"She could be a wild one, I'll grant you, but she never hurt anybody," Grandpa said. "Me and Grandma kept thinking having a baby would settle her some. Never did happen." He wiped the back of his age-spotted hand across his mouth. "Still, she had a good heart."

"I know she loved living here with you and Grandma." Her grandparents' unconditional love had given Krissy the freedom to be herself, unlike the strict regimen imposed by their workaholic parents.

But Paige had thought by the age of twenty-seven Krissy should have become a responsible adult.

Five years older than Krissy, Paige wondered if she had paid more attention to her younger sister she might have grown up better. Might have understood how to live within the restraints their parents had demanded. But by the time Paige was ten, she was helping out at the hardware store after school and weekends. At the same time, five-year-old Krissy had hated the store, hated that Mom and Dad had spent so much time there instead of catering to her demands for attention. If only Krissy had tried to think of someone besides herself.

A rush of regret assailed Paige, and she shook the thought aside. No point in dwelling on the past, as her mother would say.

"There's some leftover roast beef from last night. I could make you a sandwich. We've got more macaroni and potato salads in the fridge than we could possibly eat in a lifetime."

"You go ahead and eat something. I just don't have an appetite, child."

Paige found it endearing that Grandpa still called her a child when she'd reached the ripe old age of thirty-two. "How about coffee and a cookie or two? We ended up with plenty of those, too."

He patted her hand. "Guess I could handle that."

"It'll just take me a minute." She kissed the top of his head.

The kitchen had been updated about ten years ago with granite counters, extra-deep sinks and a double-door refrigerator. The six-burner stove ran on propane and had an oven big enough to roast two turkeys side by side. Grandma Lisbeth had loved to cook for a crowd, including the hired hands they put to work during the summer months.

The kitchen, with its long butcher block table that could seat ten and walls of walnut cabinets, was about as big as Paige's whole condo. Which, since cooking and entertaining at home weren't on her list of talents, was perfectly fine with her.

She was preparing a pot of coffee when Bryan strolled into the kitchen, letting the screen door bang shut behind him.

Paige flinched, nearly dumping coffee grounds all over the counter. She recalled there was a locked gun cabinet in the mudroom filled with rifles and shotguns. She'd never gone near those guns and hoped to goodness Grandpa was careful to keep it locked when Bryan was around.

"Jay said you were fixing something to eat." The boy was nearly as tall as Paige and whip-thin. His blond hair and delicate features made him resemble Krissy. She'd never revealed who Bryan's father was—maybe she didn't know—so there was no way to tell what genes the man had contributed to the boy's appearance.

"Grandpa isn't hungry, but I can fix you a roast

beef sandwich, and there are lots of salads crammed in the refrigerator."

"The same stuff they had at the church?"

"Yes. The ladies were very nice to let us bring the leftovers home."

He made a gagging noise. "I'll fix my own sandwich."

"Up to you. Don't you want to wash your hands first?"

He shot her a startled look. "They aren't dirty."

"You've been out there with the horses, haven't you?"

"Sure, but that's no big deal." He dragged the plate of sliced roast beef from the refrigerator and plopped it on the counter.

Her career in the hospitality business, particularly at an Elite Hotel property in Seattle, had taught her cleanliness was crucial not only for the health of the staff and guests, but for the hotel's reputation as well.

"Bryan, please. Wash your hands before touching the food." Who knew what he might have picked up in the barn or stable?

"Mom always said a few germs won't hurt anybody," he grumbled. He turned on the faucet in the sink, waved his hands under the water and turned it off. "You happy now?"

Not even close. But Paige wasn't Bryan's mother.

She needed to give him a break. The poor kid was hurting and likely looking for someone to rail against.

Assuming he had won the battle, Bryan rubbed his hands on his jeans, which looked like he'd worn them to roll around in the dirt. Paige squeezed her eyes shut. *Leave him be. You're not his mother.*

Jay chose that moment to saunter in the back door, all long legs and lean body, his old tan-colored cowboy hat perched on the back of his head. He tossed his hat on a peg in the mudroom, then walked into the kitchen. A ring of sweat made his dark hair glisten where his hat had rested.

"What are you doing, kid?" he asked.

"Fixing myself a sandwich." Bryan found a loaf of bread in the bread box, a jar of mayonnaise in the refrigerator and put them on the counter beside the plate of meat.

"Don't go messing with that stuff until you wash up," Jay said.

"I did. She saw me." He cocked his head toward Paige.

"Let me see." Jay took one of the boy's hands, turning it palm up. "Yeah, right. I've seen cowboys spit and get their hands cleaner than that. Go use some soap in the bathroom."

"Aw, come on. I'm hungry."

"You won't starve." He turned the boy by his shoulders, shoving him gently toward the half bathroom that was just inside the back door.

Bryan stomped away, his boots heavy on the hardwood floor, and slammed the bathroom door.

Paige winced. "I was going to give him a pass on his dirty hands. I know he's upset—"

"He's a kid. He needs to be told what to do."

"I thought this one time, he said his mother never—"

"Krissy probably didn't. She wasn't much for discipline." He helped himself to a couple slices of bread and a big chunk of meat.

"And you think it's okay for *you* to discipline him?"

He slathered mayonnaise on the bread. "Sure. Kids are like horses. They have to learn who's boss. They're happier if they know the rules."

Paige didn't like the idea of Jay comparing her nephew to a horse. Granted, the boy smelled like one. But he was still a child, not a horse to be broken of his bad habits.

Bryan returned to the kitchen, sullen but with clean hands.

"Get a couple plates down," Jay ordered, his tone easy and casual. "You can have this sandwich and I'll make another one for myself. Pour us both some milk, would you?"

Without balking, Bryan did as he was told.

Still holding the can of ground coffee, Paige looked on with amazement and a fair amount of admiration. Bryan appeared quite content to follow

Jay's orders. Clearly Jay knew more about raising boys than she had ever hoped to learn. Her focus on her career, and her ambition to move up to a position of manager of one of Elite Hotel's European properties didn't leave room for marriage or raising a family. Maybe someday, of course. But not in the foreseeable future.

So far no man had made an effort to tempt her to change her mind.

She watched as they sat down together to eat their sandwiches, then remembered Grandpa and the snack she'd promised him. Hurriedly, she got the coffee going and found a plate for the home-baked cookies.

She was just pouring his mug of coffee when Grandpa came into the kitchen.

"Since everybody is here, guess it's time we all had a talk." He sat at the head of the table and placed a large manila envelope beside him.

Paige delivered his coffee and cookies.

"Sit down here, child." Grandpa indicated the seat next to him. "It's important you hear what I got to say." He glanced down the table. "You, too, boy. Pay attention now."

An uneasy feeling raised the hair on her nape as Paige slipped onto the chair. Grandpa sounded so serious; something monumental must be on his mind. Could his health be failing? He seemed especially tired and stooped, which wasn't like the grandpa she knew. Maybe he was going to sell the outfitting business and retire?

"Now then, we all know that Krissy could be reckless sometimes, but she did do some planning ahead. I'll give her credit for that. 'Course, I did prod her a bit." Clearing his throat, he pulled some papers from the envelope. "Your ma loved you, Bryan. Don't you ever forget that."

The boy poked his finger into his sandwich, making a hole in the soft bread.

"After your parents passed on a few years ago, Paige, I sat Krissy down to have a long talk about Bryan."

The boy looked up. "What'd you say?"

"Hang on a minute, son. I'm getting to that." His hand shook as he took a sip of coffee. "The point is she wanted to make sure Bryan was well taken care of if something should happen to her."

A band tightened around Paige's chest. Her little sister had actually worried about what would happen to her son if she had died prematurely. Grandpa must have been very persuasive. A swell of love for him and her sister filled her chest.

"She made arrangements for Bryan?" she asked.

"Yep." Grandpa nodded and patted the papers he'd pulled out of the envelope. "She wrote out sort of a will, not that she had much money to leave to anyone. But she had her son. If worse came to worst, she wanted to be the one to name the person who'd raise her son. Be his guardian."

Paige's breath lodged in her throat. Maybe Krissy had finally named the boy's father and wanted him to care for his son. Take responsibility at long last.

Grandpa shoved the papers toward Paige. "Krissy wanted you to raise him, child. Raise him like he was your own."

Paige's mouth opened. Not a sound came out. She'd been named Bryan's *guardian*?

Why in the world—

She'd always assumed Grandpa would be there if anything—

She couldn't possibly—

Looking to the other end of the table, she realized Jay and Bryan were as shocked as she was. Both of them struck dumb.

As if the words Grandpa had spoken had finally registered, Bryan's eyes widened. His face turned red. He leaped to his feet.

"I don't want her to be my guardian!" he screamed. "I want my mom!" Knocking over his chair, Bryan raced from the room and out the back door.

Stunned, Paige sent up a heartfelt prayer. *Please, Lord, what am I supposed to do now?*

Chapter Two

Paige pushed back her chair. "I'd better go after him."

"No, I'll go." Jay stood, yanking Bryan's chair upright again. His brows and mouth drew into a disapproving scowl. "You and Henry need to talk." Grabbing his hat on the way, Jay went out the back door. The screen slammed behind him.

She exhaled. Someone really needed to fix that door.

Turning to her grandfather, Paige shook her head. "Why on earth did Krissy want me to raise her son? She and I have never been close. I hardly know Bryan, or even his likes and dislikes. It seems to me you should be Bryan's guardian. You and Grandma took care of him from the time he was born." More so than Krissy ever had, Paige suspected.

"Me and Krissy talked a lot about what to do if something happened to her. Since your folks were gone, we are the only blood relatives around."

Paige had been stunned when her parents had sold the hardware store and moved to Arizona. Competition from big-box stores had finally driven them out of business. It turned out that decision, followed by a high-speed car crash, had been a fatal one.

"Thing is, I'm getting old," Grandpa continued. "I don't have many years left. We both figured I might not be around long enough to see the boy through to being a man."

Her heart lurched. "Are you ill?"

"No, child, not that I know about anyway. And the truth is, Krissy loved you more than you might've realized." He took her hand, and she felt him tremble.

"I love...*loved* Krissy, too, Grandpa. We're sisters." An ache rose in her chest. "But I didn't really *know* her. How could I? We haven't lived under the same roof for more than a dozen years."

"I know this isn't something you expected. 'Course, Krissy didn't exactly expect to die young either, I don't suppose. But she was clear about her wishes. I told her she ought to talk to you. See if raising her boy the rest of the way would be all right with you."

"That would have at least given me some warning." Talk about being blindsided. This was as bad as a thousand good ol' boys in funny hats showing up at the hotel registration desk for a Shriners' convention that wasn't on her calendar.

If Krissy had asked, Paige would have told her right off that she wasn't prepared to be any child's parent. Certainly not a boy on the cusp of adolescence.

"I reckon she was afraid you'd say no," Grandpa said.

"I would have, Grandpa." That admission brought the heat of guilt to her cheeks. What kind of a rotten aunt did that make her? "What do I know about raising a boy? A boy who's about to be a teenager? I can't even imagine how I'd manage. And he sure wasn't keen on the idea. You saw that."

He sipped his coffee, then took a bite of a chocolate-chip cookie. "He'll adjust to the idea, given enough time."

"The way he acted, we'll both be old and decrepit before he's thrilled with the idea of me being his guardian. I'm practically a stranger to him." Granted, she should have tried harder to get to know him. But given her life, her goals, she'd have to make huge adjustments in order to do a decent job of raising him. And Bryan would have to leave everything and everyone who was familiar to him. What in the world had Krissy been thinking?

"In those papers I gave you, there's a letter from Krissy. There's probably no law that says you have to take on the boy. But maybe there's something in there that'll make you change your mind."

Paige sincerely doubted it. But could she actually

walk away from her responsibility to Bryan, her only nephew, however ill-advised Krissy's wishes might be?

Finding Bryan right where he'd expected, Jay leaned over the railing of Bright Star's stall. A palomino gelding with a blaze on his forehead, the horse had been Bryan's personal mount and his responsibility since the boy's ninth birthday.

Archie, a border collie mix that hung around the stable, rested her nose on Bryan's thigh as though she sensed the boy's distress and wanted to help. Oddly enough, when the dog had shown up a year or so ago, Bryan had started calling her Archie before he realized the dog was a girl. The name had stuck.

"You okay?" Jay asked.

Bryan lifted his head, his eyes red rimmed. He wiped his nose with his forearm. "What's all this stuff about her being my guardian?"

Jay wondered about that, too. Paige Barclay seemed the least likely person he knew to take on a half-grown kid. She hadn't looked too happy about the idea, either. Which couldn't have made Bryan feel any better.

"Guess your mom wanted to be sure you had somebody to look after you."

"Not Aunt Paige!" He tossed aside a bit of straw he'd been chewing. "She's weird. She dresses prissy and doesn't even know how to ride a horse."

Jay wouldn't call the way Paige dressed prissy. More like citified and fancier than folks around Bear Lake dressed, that was for sure, but nice. Appealing to a man's eye.

"Lots of people don't know how to ride," Jay said. Krissy had made a few snide comments about Paige's disinterest in horses. So why had she chosen her sister to be her son's guardian? A kid who lived and breathed horses? Made no sense.

"Why can't Grandpa be my guardian?" Bryan scratched Archie between her ears and got a lick of thanks in return.

"Your mom must've had her reasons." Jay couldn't figure out what they were. But then, he'd never figured out what Krissy was all about, either. "Maybe she thought Henry was too old."

"I know what we can do." The boy pushed Archie away and jumped to his feet. "You can take care of me. You're not too old."

Jay did a double take. His heart pounded in his ears. Him? The boy's guardian? Would that make sense?

"I'm not a blood relative, Bryan."

"What difference does that make? You like me, don't you?"

The boy's agitation and raised voice caused Bright Star to shift away from him. Bryan patted the horse's rump to reassure him.

"Yeah, I like you fine. But it's your mom's decision, not mine."

"Don't I get a say? I mean, isn't there somebody I can tell that I don't want prissy ol' Aunt Paige? They can't make me go off with her, can they?"

"I don't know, son." Jay had no idea what the law was about guardianship, but it did seem like Bryan was old enough to speak his mind to a judge or somebody like that. "Tell you what, there's no reason to panic. Your aunt looked as surprised as you were about your mom's request. Let's give it some time, see how everything shakes out."

"I can tell you one thing." Bryan stuck out his chin like a prizefighter challenging his opponent. "For sure I'm not moving to Seattle, if that's what she or anybody else decides. I'm staying right here with you and Grandpa and Bright Star."

Jay wasn't sure Bryan would have a choice, but he sympathized with the kid's situation. The boy's life was bound to change after his mother had tried to jump a gully that was too wide for the horse to make. She should've known better.

Even if Paige wasn't scared spitless of horses, he sensed she wouldn't ever do something that foolhardy.

A tear dropped on the letter Krissy had written to Paige. She'd brought the envelope with the letter to the room which had once been Grandma Lisbeth's sewing room. Now it served as a guest room with a narrow daybed.

Her fingers shook as she reread portions of Krissy's final message.

"I always wanted to be like you," Krissy had written in her swirling, overly dramatic handwriting.

You were so perfect, never getting into trouble like I did. Even when I tried to be good, I messed up. Like the time I dumped all the nails in one bin at the store because I thought that would look neater.

I thought Mom and Dad would love me more if I did something good for a change like you did all the time.

Paige pressed her lips together and her chin trembled as she remembered how furious their father had been. Poor Krissy hadn't realized nails came in different sizes and were separated for a reason. Neither their mother nor father had given Krissy credit for trying.

Paige had done as usual and made herself invisible in the back room. Why in the world hadn't she helped Krissy?

Because you were a coward! You didn't want your parents to be angry with you.

Finally, as time passed, Paige had realized that Krissy had stopped trying.

Paige sniffed and wiped away her tears. "I'm so sorry, Krissy," she whispered. "I should've helped you. I should've been a better sister."

Blinking, Paige continued reading the letter.

I know I used to drive you crazy by following you around. But I wanted to see how you did it, how you never seemed to get into trouble.

That's what I want for Bryan. I haven't been a real good mom, but I love my son more than I can ever say.

It just seems like I always want to see what's around the next bend in the trail, thinking maybe I'll find the answer I'm looking for somewhere out there. Fact is, I've never figured out what the right question is.

If you're reading this, it means I took a wrong trail and now Bryan really needs you. He needs your stability, the way you have your head on straight, your ambition and your goodness.

I couldn't give him those things. I don't know how. But you can. Please, Paige, take care of my son for me. I love him more than anything in the world.

I love you, too.

I know Mom and Dad would want you to do this.

Kristine

Paige gulped down a whole bucket of guilt.

Mom and Dad would want you to do this.

She blew her nose and wiped her eyes. She slipped the letter back into the envelope, which also contained a copy of Krissy's handwritten will, Bryan's birth certificate and a record of his vaccinations up to three years ago.

She'd failed her sister. Like their parents, she'd ignored Krissy's efforts to fit in, to be loved despite the fact she sometimes messed up.

Leaving the envelope on the daybed, she stepped outside onto the side porch from the sewing room.

Her grandfather owned sixty or seventy acres of land, most of it undeveloped. Paige had only explored a small portion as a child.

In the late afternoon rays of sunlight, the new needles on the pine and fir trees glistened bright green. Aspen trees down by the lake, which had shed their leaves for the winter, with the arrival of spring shimmered iridescent flashes of green in the light breeze. Not far away, Paige could hear Moccasin Creek flowing with snowmelt from the mountains that rose above Bear Lake.

Springtime was a wonderful time to be alive and a lousy time to die.

Tears sprang to her eyes again, and her vision blurred. "Why didn't you tell me all this when you were alive?"

Paige would have tried harder to get to know Krissy. Understand her.

A painful laugh broke from her throat. What a joke! Krissy had recently celebrated her twenty-seventh birthday. Paige had had all that time to help her little sister and she'd done squat.

Now she had a second chance. With Bryan. *If* he'd let her try.

It was nearly dark and Grandpa was sleeping in his recliner when Bryan finally came in the house. He marched right past Paige, who was sitting on the couch reading, and went to his room. He slammed the door.

Patience, Paige. The youngster was facing a big change in his life. Little wonder he was upset.

Grandpa mumbled something and went right back to sleep.

Sighing, Paige got up and walked down the hall. She knocked softly on Bryan's door. "It's me. Can I come in?"

"Go away!"

"I think we ought to talk, Bryan. This is all new to me, too."

Her plea was met with silence.

"Could I at least give you a hug? I know you miss your mother." She'd hugged Bryan when she had arrived yesterday, but his response had felt more perfunctory than loving. Understandable given the situation and the fact that she hadn't seen him in months.

She heard what sounded like a boot dropping to the floor in Bryan's room. A moment later, the other boot followed the first.

"Your mother loved you very much," she said to the closed door. "When she picked me to be your guardian, she thought it was the right thing to do." Paige intended to follow her sister's wishes as best she could. "Please, it won't hurt to talk, will it? I'm sure we can work things out together." That, at least, was her prayer.

The knotty-pine door remained firmly closed, the boy's displeasure radiating through the wooden barrier without the need for words.

Paige hated confrontations. She had since she'd been a child. Although she'd learned how to deal with difficult situations in her position at the hotel, she didn't think now was the time to push her luck. She'd let Bryan sleep tonight. Hopefully he'd be better able to listen and understand the situation in the morning.

Returning to the living room, she stood looking at her grandfather. There were definite signs of aging. He didn't move as fast as he used to and she'd noticed he'd become breathless walking into the church for the funeral service. She feared the difficulty was more than the stress of losing his granddaughter.

Maybe Krissy had been right not to rely on their

grandfather to see Bryan into adulthood. As much as Grandpa loved the boy, and Bryan loved him, the court might not even accept Grandpa as a viable candidate for guardian.

Too restless to read, and with no interest in checking what might be on the television, Paige decided to step outside for a breath of air and clear her head.

She retrieved her jacket from the sewing room and went out onto the front porch.

The spring air had a snap to it. She stepped off the porch and wrapped her arms around herself. The stars in the darkening sky twinkled in the clear air, a view rarely seen in Seattle. As she watched, more and more stars began to appear, each one filling its special place in the heavens.

Where was her special place? She'd dreamed of living in European capitals, caught up in their history and culture. In college she'd taken both French and German to help her achieve her goal. For the past three years, she'd used her vacation time to visit Elite Hotel properties overseas, immersing herself in the ambience, making contacts, planning her future.

In the course of one day, her future had taken a sharp turn and now included the welfare of a twelve-year-old boy.

As he headed to the barn for his last check on the horses for the night, Jay spotted Paige gazing at the stars. Cast in the faint rays of starlight, she looked vulnerable. Not the corporate executive who had shown up for her sister's funeral yesterday. More approachable. More appealing and not so standoffish.

Even though he knew it wasn't wise to test how welcoming she might be, he strolled toward her.

"How about a nickel for your thoughts?" he asked.

She started then glanced in his direction. "Is it part of your Native American thing to be able to sneak up on people?"

"Nope. My Scottish ancestors used to slip into English castles and make off with barrels of whiskey without making a sound."

The trill of her soft laughter tickled down Jay's spine. He hadn't responded to a woman's voice so strongly for a very long time.

"I gather they were well motivated," she said.

"According to the stories my great-grandfather told, fooling the British was a mark of honor in the old days."

She nodded before looking up at the sky again.

"So have you decided what to do about Bryan?" he asked.

"Krissy wanted me to be his guardian. I owe her that and more. I have to respect my sister's last wish."

Jay balled his hands into fists. That might have been Krissy's wish, but it sure wasn't Bryan's. "You're going to move him to Seattle?"

"That's where I live. Where my job is."

"Just curious, but how many horses do you own there in Seattle?"

"None, thank goodness! I live in a condo."

He pictured shoulder-to-shoulder apartments with no room to breathe, and he shuddered as much for himself as for the boy. "So there's a stable nearby where Bryan can board his horse?"

"Not that I know of. But Bryan won't need a horse in Seattle."

Jay moved a little closer and lowered his voice in frustration. "Miss Barclay, horses are that boy's life. He lives and breathes for the chance to ride the trails in the mountains. Spot a bear. Or a mountain lion. Being able to see to a horizon that's farther away than the building across the street."

She straightened her shoulders. "The city has all kinds of advantages he doesn't have here. He'll be able to go to museums, art galleries, hear a symphony orchestra. He can learn to sail on the Sound. Play any sport he likes. It's a wonderful place to live."

His jaw was going to crack, he was biting down so hard not to tell Miss Barclay exactly what he thought of that kind of life for Bryan. "You don't know a thing about raising a boy, do you?"

She backed up a step. "No, but I'm perfectly capable of learning."

Pacing away from her, Jay struggled to keep

calm. Krissy might have been reckless, but her sister was downright stubborn.

He circled back to her and got inside her personal space. "You're going to take Bryan away from all that he knows and loves and stick him in some condo with neighbors close enough to hear them brush their teeth?" Jay couldn't imagine any worse way to live, cooped up inside a building where he couldn't smell the sweet scent of spring or the biting cold of a real winter.

Not budging an inch, she planted her fists on her hips, showing more spunk than Jay thought she had. If she were a couple inches taller, she'd be right in his face. In this case, that would be a bad thing. He might just kiss her, and wouldn't that fry her beans?

"I know there will be adjustments we'll both have to make, but that's what Krissy wanted."

"And precisely what adjustments are you going make? Take weekends off so you can be home with Bryan?" He was guessing. He didn't know what her schedule was but he figured working at a hotel she had to work some crazy shifts.

Hooking her hand around the back of her neck, she hesitated. "I can't do that. I'm the conference manager for the hotel. Most of the conferences are scheduled for—"

"Fine. Then Bryan'll stay home alone. He's old enough. Of course, he won't know anyone except you. Hope you've got a lot of video games for him to play."

She folded her arms across her chest. "All right, I haven't worked out all the details yet. I just found out today—"

His jaw muscle twitched. "How big is your condo, Miss Barclay?"

"Will you stop calling me Miss Barclay?" she snapped. "My name is Paige, and I'm dealing with this guardian business the best I can."

"Okay, Paige." He shouldn't be pressing her, but the thought of her dragging Bryan off to Seattle really stuck in his craw. "You didn't answer my question about your condo."

"It's small, all right?"

"How small?" he demanded.

"One bedroom plus a home office," she admitted grudgingly. "It will do until I can sell and buy a bigger one."

"That ought to be cozy." He snatched off his old work hat and speared his fingers through his hair. She seemed to honestly believe she could take on the responsibility for a twelve-year-old, move him hundreds of miles away from the only home he'd known and everything would work itself out. Not likely!

"It's getting late." She glanced over her shoulder toward the house. "I think I'll go back inside. Good night."

"Wait!" He didn't want to stop sparring with her. Challenging her to think things through. He hadn't yet convinced her taking on parental responsibilities for Bryan wasn't such an easy thing to do. "When are you planning to leave?"

"Early Monday morning. I have to be at work Tuesday." She took a few steps toward the porch.

"You're taking Bryan with you?"

"I, um, I suppose so. I might not be able to get time off to come back."

That was crazy. Jay had to stop her. "No, you can't do that. You're not officially his guardian until a court says so."

She cocked her head. "I have Krissy's letter. That gives me the authority—"

"He only has two more weeks of school before summer vacation. You can't pull him out now. That would break his heart."

"I can't stay here for two more weeks. My boss would have a fit." Her voice tightened. "We've got a big medical conference scheduled for next weekend."

"If your boss is the right kind of guy, he'll understand. Besides, two weeks will give Bryan time to get to know you and you to get to know him." The lowered slope of her shoulders suggested he was finally getting through to her.

Hat in hand, he approached her slowly. "I understand you cared about your sister. And you care about Bryan, too. Give the boy a chance to know you, and yourself time to work out whatever steps you have to take to be his official legal guardian."

She held his gaze in the starlight for a long moment as though she wanted to say something important. Instead, her jaw tightened. "I'll think about it." Whirling, she hurried up the steps and into the house.

Jay jammed his hat on his head. He wasn't anything to Bryan except his friend. Grandpa Henry should be fighting on the boy's side. Not going along with Krissy's cockamamy idea of letting Paige raise her son.

So why was the idea of the boy moving away bugging him so much?

He thought of the son he'd lost, the tiny baby who had never drawn his first breath. The boy he'd dreamed of having. He'd planned to teach him how to ride. How to raise the best-bred quarter horses in the West. To live and work on the ranch he'd sold after Annie and the baby had died.

He'd wanted to teach his son to track animals through the woods. To hunt and fish.

But he'd never had the chance.

He scrubbed his face with his hand, remembering all of his dreams that had never come to pass. He hadn't been able to bear the thought of remaining on the ranch after he'd lost Annie. Not with all the memories that haunted him.

Bryan wasn't his own flesh and blood. But there were times, he admitted, when the kid looked at him with such—was it hero worship? Or could it be love? Despite himself, Jay had relished those moments.

However well-meaning Paige might be, he didn't want her to take Bryan away.

And he had no idea how to stop her.

Chapter Three

Jay had given Paige plenty to think about, which resulted in a restless night. Her head was still spinning with all that she had to do when she woke the next morning.

She dressed in a black wool skirt and fitted yellow sweater with three-quarter-length sleeves, and headed for the kitchen. She planned to attend church this morning. To thank the pastor again for presiding over Krissy's funeral.

Plus, she hoped with some concentrated prayer, the Lord would provide the guidance she needed.

The smell of rich coffee and the sound of male voices drew her. She stopped at the kitchen doorway and gawked. Bryan and Grandpa were sitting at the table. Jay, wearing a frilly pink apron that had to have been Grandma Lisbeth's, was cooking pancakes on the griddle. He flipped one in the air. It landed smack in the middle of the plate he was holding in his hand.

"Very impressive." She had no recollection of Jay preparing meals during any of her prior visits. Yesterday he'd already left to see to the horses when she'd come in for coffee. "You have an unexpected talent."

He shot her a grin that crinkled the corners of his eyes and sped gooseflesh down her skin. A man had to be seriously macho to carry off a pink apron with such aplomb.

"When I lead a trail ride into the wilderness, the clients expect good eats and plenty of it." He flipped a second pancake onto the plate and handed it to Bryan.

The boy grabbed the butter, slathered the pancakes, then reached for the syrup.

"Sit yourself down," Jay said. "I'll cook up a couple for you."

"No, that's not necessary. I only have coffee for breakfast."

"You're too skinny, girl." Grandpa forked a bite of pancake into his mouth. "Jay's pancakes will put some meat on your bones."

She put an affectionate hand on her grandfather's shoulder. "A woman my age has to be careful not to put too much meat on her bones."

He *harrumphed* and ate another bite of his breakfast.

"You look like you're dressed to go somewhere fancy," Jay said, pouring two more circles of batter on the griddle.

She got a mug from the cupboard and poured herself some coffee. "I thought I'd go to church this morning. Anyone like to come with me?" When no one responded, she turned to Bryan. "How about you? We could hang out."

He looked up at her with hooded eyes and shook his head.

The prick of rejection hurt. She shrugged it off. Bryan was asserting his independence. Understandable under the circumstances. Eventually he'd come around. She hoped. "How about you, Grandpa?"

"My arthritis is acting up bad this morning." He downed a gulp of coffee. "There must be a storm coming."

So far the day looked as sunny as yesterday had. But Paige knew not to challenge her grandfather's weather predictions. She remembered all too well a picnic down by the dock at the lake with her mother, grandmother and Krissy with baby Bryan. They'd ignored Grandpa's warning about the weather and he'd been right. Their picnic had been rained out.

Jay slid another plate of pancakes onto the table and sat down. "I'll drive you."

Her mouth gaped open. She hadn't expected him to volunteer to take her to church. She wasn't sure she wanted to spend time with him alone after the animosity he'd shown her last night. Besides, she was perfectly capable of driving herself.

She sat at the table opposite him. "That's all right. There's no need. I drove my car here."

He crooked a single dark brow. "No sense to take two vehicles."

"Don't you have a trail ride this morning?"

Jay swallowed his bite of pancake. "Nope. Sundays are a day of rest for us and our horses. So it's all settled. We'll go to church together."

Bossy cowboy! She closed her hands around her coffee mug, letting the heat seep in. "Fine. As long as you promise not to wear Grandma Lisbeth's apron."

He looked down at himself. Color darkened his ruddy cheeks. "Yeah, I think that's a promise I can make."

Suppressing a smile, Paige lowered her gaze. Sometimes a little teasing went a long way to smooth troubled waters. Or to gain the upper hand.

As soon as Bryan finished his pancakes, he was out the door heading for the stable and his horse.

With a grimace, Grandpa gathered himself and stood. "Think I'll go have a sit-down in the living room."

"Can I get you something for the pain?" Worried, Paige hopped up to take his elbow and walked with him into the living room.

"Don't worry your head about me, girl. A little sit-down and I'll be right as rain."

Paige didn't share his optimism. "Has the doctor given you a prescription for your arthritis?"

"Doc Johansen's not much older than Bryan and still wet behind the ears. He's as like to poison me as not. I keep my distance from that youngster. There's not much he can do anyway about me getting old, is there?" He eased himself into the recliner and let out a sigh.

Smoothing the few strands of gray hair on his balding head, Paige crouched down beside him. "Maybe I shouldn't go to church. I could stay home with you."

"Nonsense." He waved his hand like he was shooing a fly away. "I'm fine. You and Jay go on to church. It'll do you both good."

"If you're sure…"

"Go on, girl. I'll be fine."

Reluctantly, Paige agreed to leave him on his own. She'd only be gone for a couple hours at the most.

But what would happen when she returned to Seattle? Who would take care of him then? At least when Krissy was alive, she had been around to watch out for Grandpa.

When she returned to the kitchen, Jay had already put the dirty dishes in the dishwasher and cleaned up the counter. A handy man to have around.

"You ready to go?" he asked.

She checked her watch. "I guess so. I'm worried about Grandpa, though."

He glanced in the direction of the living room and lowered his voice. "He really took Krissy dying hard. He'd been pretty lively before. Now…" He shrugged. "I'll go change and meet you at my truck in ten minutes."

He strolled toward the back door and plucked his hat off the peg.

"Jay," she called after him.

He looked back over his shoulder.

"Your apron?" She worked to keep a straight face.

He rolled his eyes, yanked off his apron and hung it on the peg where his hat had been. "Ten minutes."

The screen door slammed behind him as he left.

Telling her grandfather they'd be back as soon as they could, Paige went out the front door.

Bryan was in the corral alongside a horse with a blond coat and mane. Impressed, she watched as Bryan hefted a saddle onto the horse's back, then ducked down to grab the cinch and pull it tight. He seemed to know what he was doing.

In all honesty, Paige couldn't imagine herself saddling a horse as expertly as that twelve-year-old did. Or at all. She'd be terrified the horse would step on her. Or kick her.

Bryan seemed unaware of the potential danger. That was doubly amazing considering his mother had so recently died horseback riding.

Paige bit her lip and hurried toward Jay's truck. She had to make up for the way she'd failed her sister.

It wasn't far from Grandpa's place, around the north end of Bear Lake, to Highway 93 that went through town. Although the tourist season hadn't officially started, the road was heavily traveled to and from Glacier National Park during most of the year.

Motels were mixed in between fast-food restaurants, diners and traditional businesses such as the local general store and barbershop. One cute shop, Love 2 Read Books and Bakery, had a clever caricature on the front window of a baker with a puffy white hat reading a book.

Nowhere did Paige see anything resembling an upscale resort facility with beach access to the lake. Only one restaurant, Sandy's, seemed to offer something resembling fine dining, their specialty fresh fish and steaks.

Of course, being in such close proximity to Jay distracted Paige from her survey of the town. She couldn't detect the scent of an aftershave, yet his masculine pheromones seemed to be doing a number on her, filling the truck cab and setting her on edge.

Or maybe it was his strong profile, a straight nose and determined jaw. Firm lips. Or even the way the wind blowing in the window teased his midnight-black hair, ruffling the strands like a woman's fingers. Everything about him had her thinking in ways she shouldn't.

"How come you were so excited to go to church this morning?" Jay asked. "Krissy sure didn't have any interest."

His question slammed the door on her wayward thoughts.

"Our folks didn't attend church, either. The hardware store was open seven days a week. I helped out on weekends including when I was going to college."

"That must've cut down on your social life."

As if she'd had one. "When I finally moved away from home, I found I needed…something. I started going to a small neighborhood church. I felt welcome, maybe for the first time, and loved for myself." Her cheeks flushed hot and she looked away. "That sounds hokey, doesn't it?"

"Not really."

She felt him looking at her and nausea roiled her stomach. Of all the dumb things to say, implying that she hadn't ever been loved. Of course her parents had loved her. Her teachers, too. She was the *good* sister.

"So how about you?" she asked, determined to shift the spotlight away from her. "Do you go to church regularly?"

"I try to. If I didn't, my ma would sure be on my

case. She's taught Sunday school for as long as I can remember."

"That's nice." Paige was so new to the church, she was still trying to understand the Bible and to live a Christian life "So you've always been a Christian?"

Jay rested his arm on the windowsill, hesitating a moment before he spoke. "After my wife died a few years ago, I had some trouble with God, angry at Him for letting Annie die. But He and I have worked it out."

Sympathy and a surprising surge of admiration filled her chest. "I'm sorry for your loss." She wished there was something more helpful she could say but she didn't have the words. "Your wife must have been quite young. If you don't mind talking about it, how did she die?"

His Adam's apple bobbed, the muscles of his tanned neck flexing. "Childbirth. Our son died, too."

She gasped. Her chest ached with regret that she'd been so nosy. "I'm so, so sorry. How in the world did you ever get past your anger? Losing your wife and child?"

He glanced in her direction. "I finally figured out the Lord must've known what He was doing even if I didn't. I had to trust Him."

Tears burned in her eyes. Paige had to give him extra points for experiencing such a huge loss and rebuilding his faith.

After turning off the main road, Jay asked, "So have you thought any more about Bryan and what you're going to do?"

Relieved by the shift from such an intimate, painful topic, she said, "As a matter of fact, I spent several hours on my laptop last night. You were right. Based on Montana law, even with Krissy's letter, I'll have to file a bunch of forms with the family court in order to officially become Bryan's guardian."

"I didn't think it would be easy. You can't just drag a kid off to Seattle without some kind of government rigmarole."

"Apparently that's true." Given the information she'd found online, it wasn't going to be as easy as strolling into the court in Kalispell, handing someone Krissy's letter and getting the whole deal sewed up in minutes, either. The process was going to take days, if not weeks.

"So what are you going to do? Head on back to Seattle tomorrow?"

"No. I'm not one to give up that easily. I'll drive to Kalispell tomorrow, see if there's a way I can expedite the necessary approval."

He glanced at her. "What about your boss?"

"Guess I'll have to do some fancy talking, won't I?" As much as she liked the hotel manager, she knew he wouldn't be thrilled to hear her trip to Montana had to be extended. Yet nothing critical would come up in the next day or two that her assistant couldn't handle.

"Or you could forget the guardian business and leave Bryan where he belongs."

She tensed and stared out the windshield.

Jay made the turn into the church parking lot, which was filled with pickups and SUVs, the favored means of transportation in Montana. The church itself was a simple one-story, whitewashed building with a steeple topped by a wooden cross. A welcoming place to worship the Lord.

"I can't forget about Bryan. Krissy picked me to be his guardian. For years I turned my back on her. A few phone calls to see how she was doing. Occasional visits. Presents at the holidays. Turns out all she wanted was for me to love her." Guilt rose in her throat like a boulder, cutting off her air. She swallowed painfully. "Taking care of Bryan is the one thing she's asked of me. I'm not going to say no."

He wheeled into a space next to an RV and braked hard. "Even though you know it's not what Bryan wants."

That wasn't a question, and Paige didn't respond. Somehow she'd make it work. Make Bryan see that moving to Seattle was a great opportunity. They'd develop a good relationship. A loving relationship, one she'd want with her own child if she was ever blessed with children.

And she'd have a chance to make up for the way she'd treated her sister.

Jay hopped down from the truck and went around to the passenger side to help Paige. He needn't have bothered. She'd managed on her own.

Within a few steps, however, Jay could tell walking in high heels on gravel wasn't so easy. Paige wobbled, and he caught her arm to steady her.

Slipping her arm through his, she blessed him with a tentative smile. "Thanks."

"Don't you own any shoes without high heels?"

"I have running shoes but I left them at home. I didn't expect to be gone but a few days."

He glanced at her sideways. "You run?"

"Every morning unless I'm working an early shift. I joined a twenty-four-hour gym so I wouldn't have any excuse to miss my workouts. Not even bad weather."

That news surprised Jay. Given her sophistication, he hadn't expected her to do anything more athletic than polishing her fingernails.

He glanced at her hand on his arm. Slender fingers, soft hands and nails that were cut fancy and shiny with a clear polish. Not showy but nice.

She released her grip on his arm as they reached the double-door entrance of the church. Ward Cummings, a former marine who could arm wrestle and beat anybody in town, Jay included, greeted them.

Ward handed Paige a program, then extended

one to Jay. "Good to see you, Jay. Sorry to hear about Krissy."

"Yeah. Pretty tragic." Not only for Krissy and her son, but for the horse she rode, as well. "This is her sister, Paige. Came in from Seattle for the funeral. Ward Cummings."

"I'm sorry for your loss, miss."

Paige thanked him politely before moving farther into the sanctuary.

Jay and Ward did a mock arm wrestle before shaking hands. "She's one nice-looking lady," Ward said. "How long is she going to be around?"

Jay frowned, watching Paige walk ahead of him. "Not long."

"Too bad. She'd add a little class to Bear Lake."

Yeah, maybe, he thought as he caught up with her. But classy Paige had made it clear she wasn't about to hang around Bear Lake any longer than necessary, and she sure wasn't the kind who'd have any interest in a horse wrangler who smelled of sweat and leather more times than not.

He followed her into a pew wondering what she'd meant when she'd said joining a church was the first time that she'd felt loved. What about her folks? Hadn't they loved her?

Right! They sent their other daughter away just because she got pregnant. That didn't sound like love to him.

He sat down and reached for a hymnal.

"This is a lovely little church. Very peaceful feeling." She spoke in a soft whisper than made him lean toward her, and he caught a whiff of her sweet perfume.

"I suppose it is. But sometimes if I've got a serious problem to work out, I go to a special place I found in the forest. I think of it as God's natural cathedral. Towering pines. A waterfall that ribbons down the mountain like threads of silver."

She studied him a minute, her expression intent, before she spoke. "That sounds lovely."

"If you stick around long enough, I'll take you there."

She held his gaze, her eyes a deep, warm brown. "I think I'd like that."

The organ switched from the prelude, introducing the first notes of the opening hymn. The congregation stood as Pastor Walker walked on stage and held his arms up in welcome.

Jay mentally kicked himself as he searched through the hymnal to find the right page. Why had he offered to take Paige to the spot where he went when he needed to pray? His private place of contemplation. A place where he felt closer to Annie.

He didn't want to take someone like Paige there, a woman who didn't want anything to do with him or his beloved horses.

As he held out the open hymnal to Paige, he realized he didn't have to worry. She would turn down

the invitation the instant she learned the only way
to get to his cathedral was on horseback.

Grandpa had been right about a storm coming.

By afternoon, clouds had filled the sky, bringing
with them an early twilight. Rain spattered on the
roof and dimpled the worn path from the barn to
the house. Inside, a cozy fire snapped and crackled
in the natural-stone fireplace.

Grandpa was reading a newspaper. Bryan lay
sprawled on the floor in front of the fire playing a
game on an electronic device.

Pondering how she could break through Bryan's
reticence and make a connection with him, Paige sat
down at the upright piano. She ran her fingers over
the keys, running up and down the scales. She'd
taken lessons and played all through high school,
often accompanying the choir or student musicals.

"Hey, Bryan," she said. "Remember when we
used to play 'Chopsticks' together?"

He turned to look at her. "Uh-uh."

"Don't you remember this?" Using two fingers,
she tapped out the familiar tune. "You got pretty
good at it."

She had his attention enough that he took the ear
buds out of his ears. *A tiny bit of progress.*

"You played the melody and I played the accompaniment." She struck the appropriate chords, im-

provising a few swirling runs. "Come on. Let's try it together."

"I don't remember how."

"I'll show you again."

Grandpa folded his newspaper. "Go on, boy. Give it a try."

Reluctantly, Bryan got up. He walked to piano and sat on the bench next to her. She caught a whiff of wood smoke and little boy sweat, and smiled.

"Watch the keys I play, and you play the same ones an octave higher. Like this." She demonstrated slowly, then asked him to try. He came close to getting it right and they practiced again.

When she thought he was ready, she let him set the beat and added the accompaniment.

They made it all the way through the song. "Magnificent!" she cheered. She held up her hand for a high five.

He looked startled, then grinned and slapped her hand.

A beginning, she thought. *From little things, big things can grow.*

Glancing toward Grandpa, she discovered Jay leaning one shoulder against the kitchen doorway watching her. His brows were lowered in disapproval, his lips a straight line.

Jay didn't believe she could make a good life for Bryan. She did. For Krissy's sake, and with God's help, she would.

Chapter Four

"You don't have to walk me to the bus."

Walk? Paige was having to run to keep up with Bryan, who charged ahead of her to catch the school bus.

"I thought it would be fun to see how you got to school." Of all the things she hadn't brought with her, the absence of her running shoes was, at minimum, going to cost her a broken ankle.

"What fun?" He increased his pace, his backpack slung over his shoulder. "It's a yellow bus. Big deal."

"Bryan, slow down." This was not the way she had envisioned starting her first Monday morning as Bryan's sort-of guardian. "Let's walk together."

He halted and whirled toward her, scowling. "Aunt Paige, don't you know the guys are gonna rag on me if they see you walking me to the bus like I was a little kid?"

"Oh." She stopped. Swallowed hard. "I guess I wasn't thinking."

"Yeah, I guess you weren't." He turned and continued down the dirt road.

She didn't follow him. Thoroughly chastised, she called after him. "Have a nice day."

He didn't bother to acknowledge her good wishes.

Sighing, she turned back toward Grandpa Henry's house. She strolled along the side of the road, in no hurry now.

It's not like anyone had prepared her to be Bryan's guardian. They hadn't given her a how-to book either. This trial-and-error business was going to be painful for both of them.

As soon as she got Bryan settled in Seattle, she'd have to arrange for family counseling. The two of them needed to learn to communicate better. Bryan would probably need some help dealing with his grief and the changes in his life.

The storm had passed through last night, leaving only a few puffy clouds in the early morning sky. Residual rainwater puddled the dirt road and oozed into the depressions left by her high heels. Jay Red Elk wouldn't have any trouble tracking her, if he was interested. Which was unlikely.

She'd have to call her boss in Seattle, Mr. Armstrong, and tell him about the newest life-changing event since the death of her sister. Then she'd drive to Kalispell and try to deal with the guardianship arrangement.

Pausing, she watched a bee flitting around a

cluster of blue lupine in a sunny area. She remembered Grandma Lisbeth knew the names of all the wildflowers in the area but Paige hadn't bothered to remember them. Now she wished she'd paid more attention.

She looked up and her breath caught. Off to the side of the road in the shade of a stand of pine trees stood two white-tail does and their fawns, who couldn't be more than a few weeks old. They still had their spots like two young Bambi look-alikes. The does eyed Paige suspiciously then moved farther into the woods with their precious babies.

Their beauty and dignity, their natural mothering instincts, touched something in Paige's heart. Could she learn to be that good a mother for Bryan?

She could only pray she would, in time, learn how to give him all the love he needed.

As she approached the corral, she saw Jay saddling a horse.

He tipped his hat to her. "So you saw Bryan to the school bus?"

"Not exactly."

He quirked his lips in what had to be an I-told-you-so grin. "He wasn't too pleased to have his buddies see you playing mama?"

"Something like that." She cringed, realizing he'd seen her trailing after Bryan like a stray dog.

"Kids can be sort of touchy about adults hanging around them," he said.

Paige should have known that. But with her parents, she'd always done exactly what they had asked of her. If they came to a performance of the sixth grade class, she was thrilled. And that only happened if the hardware store could close early. She'd longed for her parents' attention almost as much as Krissy had. The only way Paige could gain their praise was to excel at the hardware store.

A black-and-white dog with floppy ears trotted over to greet Paige. Noticing the dog was a bit plump, she knelt to pet him.

"Oh, aren't you a good boy." His tail wagged enthusiastically. "What's his name?"

"That's Archie," Jay said. "He's actually a she. Bryan sort of misnamed her, but it stuck anyway. She keeps the horses company, the coyotes away and lets us know if there's a bear around."

She popped to her feet. "There are bears here?"

"Not right now. If there were, Archie would be barking her head off."

Taking a quick look up the hillside, Paige felt only marginally reassured by Jay's comment.

"Archie's also pregnant," Jay said.

"Really? I did think he...*she* was getting plenty to eat." She'd never owned a dog. Too much trouble, her mother had insisted. She imagined seeing newborn puppies would be quite a treat.

She edged closer to the corral, Jay and his horse, feeling safe with the sturdy fence between her and the animal. The way the horse watched her with those big brown eyes unsettled her. When he raised his head and nodded twice, she wondered what he was thinking and how far away she should stand from those big teeth of his.

"What kind of a horse is that?" She had to admit his chestnut coat was the reddish-brown shade of hair color many women spent big bucks to achieve.

"A quarter horse." Jay flipped the stirrup up onto the saddle and reached for the cinch. "Best all-around riding horse there is." Pride lifted his words.

"Does he have a name?"

"Thunder Boy."

"That sounds ominous."

Resting his arm across the saddle, Jay chuckled. "He's harmless. The way he's nodding at you means he wants you to say hello and pat his nose."

She took a step back. "That's okay. No need for introductions."

His smile recast itself into a scowl. "Paige, if you want to get to know Bryan better, you're going to have to make friends with horses. They aren't going to hurt you."

She folded her arms across her chest. "One of them killed my sister."

"Krissy did that to herself."

If Jay's comment was meant to make her feel more comfortable around Thunder Boy, or any other horse, it wasn't working.

He patted the horse's neck, pulled something from his shirt pocket and stepped up to the fence. "Here." He held out his hand. "Thunder really likes apples. Why don't you feed him a piece?"

Paige gaped at the quartered apple. "I don't think so."

As agilely as a gymnast, Jay boosted himself over the corral and landed beside Paige. "We'll feed him together. Come on." Taking her hand, he opened her fingers and placed the apple on her palm. "Thunder will be your friend forever. I promise."

Ripples of panic swam through her midsection. "No, really."

Despite her refusal, he put her open hand on his palm. His warmth, the feel of his wide callused hand beneath hers, seemed to transmit a dose of the courage she'd always lacked. The sensation spread up her arm, blocking out her fears and her good sense.

Thunder bent his head over the top railing toward her hand.

"Steady now," Jay crooned, either to Thunder or Paige, she wasn't sure which.

Thunder's big lips parted, revealing huge teeth. Paige almost bolted. But the horse kissed her palm with those lips in the gentlest of touches, testing the apple, then lifting it into his mouth.

Paige blinked, studied her palm, which was still intact and looked small in Jay's much larger hand. She met his blue-green gaze. "His lips are so soft."

Jay's mouth tilted at the corners. "Soft as…" His thumb caressed her palm. "As soft as your hand." He'd lowered his voice to a deep, masculine timbre that rolled through his broad chest.

Still gazing into his eyes, she slowly withdrew her hand.

"I've got another piece of apple if you want to try it again," he said, his voice tempting her.

"I, um, I have to call my boss." As if Jay were a magnet holding her close, it took all of Paige's mental concentration to move away from him.

"Another time, then." He touched the brim of his cowboy hat.

"Yes. Maybe. We'll see." Breathless, her heart racing, she hurried toward the main house. It had to be the altitude that made her feel off-kilter. The cool, crisp mountain air. Clearly, as soon as possible, she needed to return to Seattle and sea level where she'd be able to catch her breath again.

Thunder Boy nudged Jay's shoulder looking for another treat. He rubbed the horse's velvety nose.

"Okay, boy, you earned it." Chuckling a bit, Jay palmed his last piece of apple. "Thanks for not biting her."

Thunder lipped the apple into his mouth and nodded his appreciation.

Jay had met few people who were as afraid of horses as Paige Barclay was. Even fewer who had softer hands or who smelled so sweet. Like a bunch of honeysuckle growing alongside the trail. Impossible not to miss the perfume after you'd ridden on by.

He'd felt her tremble when he had taken her hand. Was that from fear? Or from something else?

He climbed back over the fence and untied Thunder's reins. His job was to check out the trail to Arrowhead Cove, see if it was clear of winter debris, fallen trees or washed-out areas. He wasn't supposed to lollygag around thinking about a woman with soft hands and a fear of horses.

It would be better if he could come up with a way to make her realize she wasn't a suitable guardian for a twelve-year-old boy who loved horses.

Not suitable for Jay, either. Every inch of Paige Barclay shouted she wanted to return to the city. She belonged there.

Mounting, he turned Thunder toward the corral gate.

As he walked his horse past the big house, he spied Paige's footprints in the soft ground leading up onto the front porch.

That woman really ought to get down to the general store and buy a pair of boots suitable for walking around the grounds and stable at Bear Lake Outfitters. Those high heels she wore might look fine on her and were okay for traipsing around on plush carpet in a fancy hotel, but not out here on the ranch.

But mountain country was different. She needed to learn that. Or go back home.

She'd tracked mud clear across the front room.

Leaning against a wall, she took off her heels and stood in her stocking feet. Mud caked her shoes, ruining them.

At the very least she'd have to start using the mudroom. And find some more appropriate shoes—and clothes—for whatever length of time she'd be here at Bear Lake.

She walked down the hallway to Krissy's room. Guilt and regret, mixed with a trace of anger, assailed Paige as she reached the closed-off bedroom. Sisters should be close. Best friends. Someone with whom to share hopes and dreams.

That had never been the case between Paige and her sister.

Had it been Paige's fault? Or Krissy's? Or both to some degree?

Perhaps it was the five-year difference in age that had made it so difficult for them to communicate.

Taking a deep breath, Paige opened the bedroom door. She imagined Krissy was there, playing a game of hide-and-seek as she'd loved to do as a child. Any moment she'd jump out trying to frighten Paige.

The fact that wasn't going to happen ever again

stoked an ache in Paige's chest that felt like a red-hot poker.

She drew a painful breath and looked around. The room shouted that a determined tomboy lived here. One who was far from being neat and tidy.

A black-and-white striped quilt had been carelessly thrown across the double bed. Photos of horses, cowboys and western scenes covered the walls. Clothes had been tossed unmindfully on a maple rocking chair; shoes and boots were left where they had fallen.

Paige shuddered, comparing her pristine and orderly condo where she rarely left anything out of place with her sister's living space. One thing was clear, they would have driven each other crazy if they had been roommates.

A few years ago when Paige had been visiting, she and her sister had gone shopping together in Missoula, the largest town around, two hours south of Bear Lake. Their taste in clothes was so opposite, the trip was pretty much a disaster.

Feeling like she was snooping, Paige opened the walk-in closet door. Granted she and her sister were built differently—Krissy with a far more feminine figure than Paige's almost nonexistent curves. Still, there might be a pair of jeans that would fit and maybe boots.

The thought of wearing her sister's clothes made Paige feel ghoulish, but she wasn't going to be here long. Her finances were such that she didn't want to waste a lot of money buying new clothes she'd probably never wear after she returned to Seattle.

The closet wasn't any better organized than the room. Clothes were hung in random order, jeans next to silk blouses, sundresses stuck in wherever there was room. The closet floor was a jumble of shoes and boots and fallen garments.

Kneeling, she pawed through the pile of shoes. She found one red tennis shoe, only a half size bigger than Paige wore. Now, if she could only find the matching one.

When she uncovered that, she dug in to find a pair of boots that might work for her. After that she searched for jeans. The ones she tried on were a bit baggy, but they would do for the next few days.

Taking a deep breath, she looked around Krissy's room. The thought of clearing out and disposing of all of her sister's things knotted in her stomach. She'd have to talk to Grandpa. And Bryan, she realized. It might be better to leave things as they were until the shock of losing Krissy had faded.

Surely there was no rush, and for Bryan's sake, Paige didn't want to erase the memory of his mother.

Returning to her room, Paige got the paperwork together that she needed to file for Bryan's guardianship.

Then she called her boss. As she expected, Mr.

Armstrong was not thrilled with the news that her return to Seattle would be delayed.

After the eighty-mile round trip to Kalispell, plus an hour dealing with the court clerk and filing her request to be Bryan's guardian, Paige was tired and hungry.

As she drove by the barn, through the wide open door she noticed a young man and Grandpa inside. Parking in front of the house, she grabbed Krissy's red tennis shoes, slipped them on and got out of the car. She left her high-heel pumps on the front seat.

The smell of hay and animals struck her as she walked into the barn. Several bales of hay were stacked by the open door. Nathan, a lanky twenty-something, hefted a bale and carried it inside.

Sitting to the side near the tack room, Grandpa was working on a saddle. She caught the scent of ammonia and saddle soap.

"Hi, Grandpa. How are you feeling?"

He glanced up at her. "I'm fine, child. How'd your trip to Kalispell go?"

"All right, I guess."

"Kalispell is too citified for me." Grandpa went back to rubbing the leather saddle. "All those people and cars make me nervous."

She laughed. "I guess you won't be coming to visit me and Bryan in Seattle then."

"Nope. Don't imagine so."

She suppressed a sudden pang of dismay. Driving to Seattle on his own would be too far, too hard, for Grandpa.

He nodded. "It'll be quiet around here with both him and Krissy gone, that's for sure."

She swallowed hard. She hadn't given any thought to how much Grandpa would miss Krissy and Bryan. He'd seemed so supportive of her becoming Bryan's guardian. She'd wanted to please him. Maybe the reality had finally sunk in.

"Did you have any lunch, Grandpa?"

"Yep. Jay made us a couple sandwiches."

Grateful that Jay had looked out for Grandpa, she said, "I didn't take time to eat on the way home, so I'm going to find something for myself."

"I could use a glass of iced tea, if you've got the time," Grandpa said.

"Sure. I'll be back in a minute with a pitcherful. Nathan might want some, too."

She walked out of the barn. Momentarily blinded by the bright sun, she bumped smack into the solid wall of Jay's chest.

"Hey, nice shoes," he said, steadying her.

Heat rushed to her cheeks. Why in the world did he always show up out of nowhere? And why did she react with a strange quivering sensation deep inside?

She regained her footing and her mental equilibrium, and took a step away from him. "The shoes were Krissy's. They're a half size too big, but I had to do something."

"Smart girl! Better than breaking your neck." He thumbed his hat back. "So what happened in Kalispell?"

"They gave me a court date for the hearing about Bryan."

His eyes narrowed. "When?"

She bristled at his sharp-edged tone. "Unfortunately, the soonest date they could give me is the end of next week. I think I'll go back to Seattle this Thursday. I'll be there for the medical conference at the hotel over the weekend, which will please my boss. I'll also be able to start setting things up for Bryan."

"So you'll have what, four days this week to get to know him? Then you'll duck out and reappear just in time to drag him back to Seattle with you?"

"You were the one who said he shouldn't miss the last two weeks of school." She pointed her chin at him. "Now you get your way and you're angry about it. Why's that?"

His blue-green eyes darkened to almost black. His jaw muscle jumped and his Adam's apple bounced.

"If you're going to have any kind of a relationship with that boy, you'd better spend every minute you can with him before you go off to Seattle."

"Fine. I'd be happy to. But just how am I going to

do that when he spends all of his time in the barn or stables or off somewhere on his horse?"

"Then I guess you're going to have to get up close and personal with his horse." He squared his hat, gave her another hard look and strode past her into the barn.

She fumed. Had he forgotten her fear of horses? Or had he said that to point out what a terrible guardian she'd be for Bryan?

Well, forget that, Mr. High-and-Mighty. It might take some time and effort, but she and Bryan would be fine.

Jay snatched up a bridle that needed to be cleaned, grabbed a sponge and dipped it in the ammonia-laced water. That fool woman had no right to take Bryan away. He belonged here at Bear Lake Outfitters, not in some dinky condo in Seattle.

"You act like a man with a problem," Grandpa Henry said.

Jay scrubbed the bridle to get rid of accumulated dirt and grime, a chore that needed doing once a week to all the tack to keep it in good shape.

"How come you're okay with Bryan moving to Seattle?" he asked.

Henry worked the saddle soap into the leather in slow, patient circles. "It's what Krissy thought was right. Paige was her sister. Family counts."

"Yeah, but you're his great-grandfather. You're

family." Jay wasn't. Never could be. "He could've stayed here. Together we could've looked after him."

"Guess when Krissy and me were talkin', it didn't occur to either of us that she'd actually die before I did. Before the boy was grown. That sure didn't seem real to me. Still doesn't."

"If you had it to do over, would you have told her to pick Paige for Bryan's guardian?"

Setting his cleaning rag aside, Henry hefted the saddle, carried it into the tack room and set it in its floor stand.

"I didn't tell her. She decided. Don't much matter now, does it? What's done is done."

Jay didn't particularly like that answer, but he didn't know what else he could do.

A few minutes later, Paige came sauntering into the barn carrying a tray with a pitcher of iced tea and three glasses.

Jay gaped at her. She was wearing jeans that were belted, emphasizing her slender waist and the slight swell of her hips. On her feet she wore scuffed cowboy boots. She might be a city girl, but in that outfit she looked like she belonged right here in Montana high country.

He shook the thought off. Jeans and boots didn't change a person on the inside.

"We still had a few cookies left," she said, after filling the glasses with tea. She extended the plate of cookies to her grandfather. "Thought you might like them with your tea."

Smiling, he selected an iced cookie. "That's thoughtful of you, child."

She offered the cookies to Jay.

Leaning against the doorjamb of the tack room, he met her gaze as he leaned against the doorjamb of the tack room. The cookies weren't a peace offering. She was still mad at him. He saw the spark of determination in her eyes. In spite of himself, he admired her decisiveness. "Thanks."

"You're welcome."

She delivered cookies to Nathan, who in his quiet fashion was sitting on a nearby bale of hay, and finally took one for herself. "I'll leave the rest of the cookies and the pitcher of tea for you. I have to call my boss, let him know that I'll be there for the—"

Bryan came running into the barn, home from school. "Hey, Grandpa. Jay. Guess what?" He spotted Paige and slid to a stop.

"Hi, Bryan. What's up?" she asked.

The boy glanced between Jay and his grandfather. "I was going to tell 'em that Game Day is gonna be this Friday."

"That's great, son," Grandpa said. "You can count on me being there."

"Me, too," Jay said.

A frown wrinkled Paige's forehead. "What's Game Day?"

"It's a school thing," Jay explained. "They have races, tug-of-war…the classes compete against each other."

"Yeah, and I'm one of the fastest guys in my class," Bryan bragged. "I'm gonna beat Toby this year. I'm gonna win the baseball toss, too. You get medals and stuff for winning."

"Wow, that sounds exciting," Paige said. "I'd like to come cheer you on, too. Is that okay with you?"

Bryan twisted his lips. "Yeah, I guess so," he mumbled.

Jay stepped away from the doorjamb. "I thought you had to be someplace else on Friday."

She turned and looked him straight in the eye. "I can't think of anyplace in the world that I'd rather be than watching Bryan win a whole bunch of medals at Game Day."

Mentally, Jay kicked himself. Looked like Paige was taking this getting-to-know-Bryan business seriously. Maybe he should've kept his mouth shut.

On second thought, implementing plan A would still work. Getting her to recognize how ill-suited she was to be the guardian of a boy who lives and breathes horses should be easy.

Except he suspected nothing about Paige was easy.

Chapter Five

Thinking she'd one-upped Jay for a change, Paige turned to leave, then thought of a better idea.

"Are you hungry, Bryan? I saw some apples in the refrigerator if you'd like a snack. I could make you a peanut butter and jelly sandwich."

Looking like he was going accept her offer, Bryan shrugged.

"You've got chores to do, kid," Jay reminded him. "Bright Star's bridle and saddle need cleaning."

"Yeah, I know. I'll do it after I eat somethin'."

Smugly, Paige realized the way to a growing boy's heart was through his stomach.

Jay put his empty iced-tea glass on the tray. "Fine. Maybe your aunt Paige will help you clean Star's tack."

Cocking her head, Paige went still for a moment trying to figure out what Jay was up to. "I guess I could do that," she replied cautiously. "It's like polishing shoes and silverware, right?"

"Pretty much," Jay said. "When you're done cleaning the tack, Bryan can teach you how to saddle his horse."

"Huh? Me?" Bryan's expression went blank.

"Yeah, you. You're a whiz at saddling a horse, aren't you?"

"I guess." Bryan shot a puzzled look in Paige's direction then headed out of the barn.

Paige's mouth went dry, and her heart lurched an extra beat, hard enough that she placed her hand on her chest to prevent its escape. A cold sweat crept down the back of her neck.

Saddling a horse meant getting close to the horse. Very close.

Smart-aleck, arrogant cowboy! He'd boxed her into a corner. There was no way she could get out of his trap. She didn't want Bryan to think she was a wimp. Even if she was.

Jay picked up his cleaning cloth and winked at her before turning away to find another bridle to polish.

A primitive scream rose in her throat. She bit down hard to keep it locked inside.

Forget his macho cowboy ways. How his hat shadowed his eyes, making him seem mysterious. His broad shoulders. The way his lips quirked when he thought something was funny.

Someday she'd get back at Jay Red Elk for his sneaky tricks. She'd make him eat his words that she wasn't a suitable guardian for Bryan.

Nearly an hour later, per Bryan's instructions, Paige carried a decidedly smelly saddle blanket out of the barn. Bryan handled the saddle. Bright Star, a pretty blond horse, stood tied to a railing in the shade of the barn. He lifted his head at Bryan's approach and nickered. Bryan rested the saddle on the railing.

Paige halted several feet away.

"Okay, go ahead, Aunt Paige. Put the blanket on his back."

Her knees rubbery, she took a tentative step forward but kept herself at arm's length. In her imagination, she saw herself as a child falling out of the saddle. The sudden pain when she'd landed. And the terror she'd felt when the horse nearly stepped on her.

She drew in a deep breath.

And tossed the blanket toward Bright Star.

The blanket bounced off the horse and slipped to the ground. Paige groaned.

Bright Star skittered sideways, his eyes wide.

Somewhere behind her she heard a choked laugh. *Jay's laugh!*

"Aunt Paige!" With a disgusted look, Bryan walked right up to the horse, gave him a reassuring pat on his neck, and picked up the blanket. "You can't *throw* the blanket at him. You gotta put it on his back like this." He demonstrated.

"Oh, I see." Her voice quavered.

The boy pulled the blanket off. "Come on, try it again." He held out the blanket to her.

"I…" She felt Jay watching her. Knew the smug expression she'd see if she turned around to look at him. "I'm sorry. I'm just a little nervous."

"That's okay. I was kinda nervous the first time my mom put me on a horse."

"How old were you?"

"I dunno. Three or four, I guess."

She was thirty-two and had less courage than a three-year-old. Sweat edged down between her breasts. Her leg that had been broken so long ago started to ache, a phantom pain, at the thought of getting up close and personal with the horse.

Bracing herself, she took the blanket. Bryan held Bright Star by the halter.

With great care, she placed the blanket on the horse's back. He shifted from one foot to another, and Paige quickly stepped away.

Bryan scooted the blanket up a bit on Bright Star's neck. "Okay, now get the saddle. I already hooked up the stirrups and cinches so they'd be out of your way."

She eyed the saddle. She'd managed to get the

blanket on the horse. How hard could it be to put a saddle on top of the blanket?

Except she'd underestimated how heavy it was. Bryan was only twelve and pretty skinny, but he had hauled the saddle out here without any trouble.

As she struggled to carry the saddle, one of the stirrups came undone. She grabbed for it, juggling the awkward load in her arms and shoving it up onto her shoulder. With a grunt, she launched the saddle across Bright Star's back.

The blanket slid out from under the saddle and fell off to the other side. A stirrup whacked her in the face at the same time Bright Star kicked out with his rear legs.

Panic drove Paige backward. Her oversize boots slipped on something and she landed hard on her rear end.

Jay's male laughter burst from the barn, joined by Bryan's younger, high-pitched voice hooting and hollering at her expense.

Something snapped inside Paige. She scrambled to her feet and held up her hand like a crossing guard to stop Jay, who was hurrying toward her. Tears of embarrassment burned in her eyes. Fury scorched her cheeks. *Now he wants to help? Forget that!*

"All right, cowboy." She glared at Jay, who seemed to be trying hard not to laugh, but he couldn't keep the smile off his face. Grandpa and

Nathan were standing in the barn doorway, grinning like fools.

"I'd like to see you plan a reception for nine hundred doctors who scarf up hors d'oeuvres like popcorn because they're too cheap to buy their own dinner and their conference coordinator underestimated attendance by twenty percent. And that's after you've spent the whole afternoon rearranging their room assignments because they didn't want the morning sun to bother them or they'd brought their kids with them and hadn't bothered to mention that little detail when they made their reservation."

"I'm sorry." Tamping down his grin, Jay waved his hand as though he could silence her so easily. "Really, I didn't mean—"

"And in the middle of all that, some overweight doctor, who should know better, has a heart attack and you've got to clear the room, get the defibrillator out of the first aid room, call 9-1-1, then—"

"I know, I know. I'm sorry." He wiped his hand across his mouth and blew out a breath.

"You put the saddle on backward, Aunt Paige," Bryan announced, still laughing.

"That's enough, son," Jay said, silencing the boy.

She whirled and narrowed her eyes. Sure enough, the saddle horn faced toward the rear of the horse. How in the world had she done that?

Jay came up beside her, looping his arm around her shoulders. "You're absolutely right. There's no way I could handle your job. I'd probably close the hotel down tight and send 'em all home."

"Management wouldn't exactly approve of that," she muttered.

"Yeah, I wouldn't last long, would I?"

His arm felt so right around her, his reassuring tone as comforting as a warm winter sweater, she almost forgot how mad she was at him for laughing. Almost!

And the truth was, she must have looked plain silly trying to get that saddle on backward.

"You want to try again, Aunt Paige?"

No!

"I think your aunt has had enough of horses for today," Jay said. "You go ahead and saddle him up. Take him for a ride to calm him down."

Bryan lost no time removing the misplaced saddle and scooping up the blanket to start over.

"I guess I'm a real dunce, aren't I?" she said.

"Nope. It was your first time. Anybody would be nervous." The corners of his lips quivered.

Paige was pretty sure Jay had never been anxious or nervous about anything in his life, including rattlesnakes, mountain lions and going to his high school prom. She'd dreaded them all.

His arm still around her, Jay escorted Paige back into the barn.

"You all right, child?" Grandpa asked.

"Outside of making a complete fool of myself, I'm fine."

"You got spunk, child. No doubt about that."

She'd need a lot more than spunk to prove to Jay—and Bryan—that she was worthy of being anyone's guardian.

When Bryan came back from his ride, Jay had a talk with him.

"I know your aunt looked pretty funny with that saddle business," he said as Bryan led Bright Star into his stall. "But we shouldn't laugh at people who make mistakes."

The boy looked up at him. "You were laughing."

"Yeah, I know. But I was trying really hard not to." Which hadn't been easy. "And I'm going to apologize again at supper. Maybe you should too."

Bryan scrunched up his face.

"She was trying because of you, son."

"Because of me?"

"She really wants you to like her. She's trying real hard to get to know you."

"Okay." He shrugged his shoulders. "I'll tell her I'm sorry."

"Good boy!" Jay gave him an encouraging pat on the back.

By the following morning, Jay had to hope Bryan had had better luck saying he was sorry than he had.

During dinner he had tried to apologize again. She'd wanted none of it. Nearly silent while they ate, she'd retreated to her room after cleaning up the kitchen.

She'd been equally quiet this morning, finally announcing that after Bryan left for school, she was going to the grocery store.

Now, as he and Nathan gathered horses in the corral for the morning trail ride, a flock of wild turkeys gobbled their way along the dirt road. A morning dove cooed from the top of the barn.

Paige wasn't the talkative kind like those silly turkeys. She was more like the dove, soft and innocent. Defenseless against the way Jay had set her up for failure trying to saddle Bright Star. He worried how he could to make it up to Paige for what he'd done. He shouldn't have pressed her so hard. He'd known she was scared.

Effectively throwing her into the deep end had been cruel. He was usually a better man than that. He imagined Annie would have given him what for if she'd been around.

Paige had torn into him, too, as rightly she should have. All riled up, she was a fiery, beautiful woman. No wonder Henry thought she had spunk.

So what had gotten into Jay? It wasn't Paige's fault Krissy had named her as Bryan's guardian.

Working next to Jay, Nathan hefted a saddle onto

a mixed-breed gelding named Aladdin, a good trail horse who liked to be at the front of the pack.

"What kind of riders have we got this morning?" Nathan asked.

"It's two families, total of seven including three kids. One of them hasn't ridden before."

"Hope none of 'em are as scared as Miss Barclay is," the young wrangler commented. "That was sure funny how she got the saddle on backward. Never did see a thing like that before." He chuckled. "If Bryan hadn't been hanging on, poor Bright Star would've taken off all the way to Moose Peak on his own."

Jay grimaced. "It wasn't funny to Miss Barclay, so keep your chuckles to yourself."

"Yes, sir." Quickly sobering, Nathan pulled the front cinch up tight to hold the saddle in place.

"Let's saddle Peaches for the kid who hasn't ridden before." Peaches was a pretty little paint with brown-and-white markings and a good disposition. Since Jay had been caring for Henry's string of horses, Peaches had put up with a lot of untrained riders and had never shown a bit of temper.

That was the horse he should've introduced to Paige. The gentle little mare wouldn't have intimidated her in the first place. At least if Jay had been there protecting Paige, helping her, going slow, she would've been okay.

He wondered if she'd be willing to try again, this time with him by her side.

Jay had the trail riders back to the stables by noon. There were lots of moans and groans as the inexperienced riders discovered they'd used muscles they hadn't known existed. But they were happy, particularly since they'd caught sight of a group of deer and had spotted a pair of ospreys putting the finishing touches on their nest high up in the snag of a cedar tree.

After seeing that the horses were watered, fed and cooled down, Jay went into the main house. Paige's car was out front, so he knew she was home.

He found her in the kitchen cleaning up the dishes from Henry's lunch and her own. She had on one of Krissy's T-shirts, which hung loosely on her.

She glanced in Jay's direction. "I didn't know when you'd be back. I put a sandwich in the refrigerator for you, if you're hungry."

He smiled, pleased she was at least speaking to him. "Thanks. I'm always hungry." Opening the refrigerator, he found a covered plate with a ham sandwich, tomato and lettuce on the side.

"There's mustard if you want it. I didn't know—"

"I got it." He held up the plastic container.

"Then you're all set." She dried her hands on a paper towel and started toward the living room.

"Paige, wait. Sit and talk with me. Please."

She halted and looked back over her shoulder, her expression wary.

"I really am sorry about what happened yesterday. And that I laughed. Can we call a truce?" He held up his hand, palm out.

When some of the tension went out of her shoulders, he gestured toward a chair at the table.

"We both care about Bryan and Grandpa, and want the best for them," she said, sitting down and placing her delicate hands on the table. She fussed with her fingers as though checking her nail polish. "It seems to me we should be on the same side."

Jay slid into his chair. He would agree with her except she was going to take Bryan to Seattle.

He spread some mustard on the sandwich and piled on the tomato and lettuce. "I still think it'll work out best for Bryan if you two spend some time getting to know each other. And the best way for you to do that is to understand how he feels about horses."

"I'd say my attempt at doing that was an abject failure, wouldn't you?"

"That wasn't your fault. I let you get in over your head. I should've started you off easier. Something simple, so you wouldn't be afraid."

"I'm a grown woman. I shouldn't be terrorized by a horse."

"No, you shouldn't, but the fact is, you are. So we'll start again. You can get over your fear if we work at it." When she shook her head, Jay figured he'd lost the argument. Angry at himself, he bit into the sandwich.

Sighing audibly, she said, "What did you have in mind?"

Smiling around his mouthful, he nodded and swallowed. "Attagirl. I knew you weren't a quitter."

She cocked an eyebrow, a cute expression that said she was wary but willing to listen. He appreciated a woman who was open to hearing his opinion. Idly he wondered if anyone had kissed that clever eyebrow and how she had reacted.

"I want you to get to know Peaches," he said.

Both of her brows jumped up. "Your girlfriend?"

He chuckled. "No, but she is the sweetest thing around here on four legs. Peaches is a pinto. Wonderful disposition. You'll like her."

"Another horse? Jay, I'm simply not sure—"

"Remember, you're doing this for Bryan's sake."

"I'd just as soon he not see me making a fool of myself again."

"Which is why, as soon as I finish this sandwich, we're going to go meet Peaches."

Her enthusiasm for the idea was equal to that of someone about to be hanged from the nearest tree.

Paige stood back from Peaches's stall wondering why it was so important for her to learn anything about horses. It wasn't like she ever intended to own one, or even go for a ride on one. She understood Bryan would miss his horse after he moved to Seattle, but he'd find other activities to enjoy. She hoped.

Jay stepped into the stall with Peaches, patted her neck and rubbed his hand over her nose.

"Pretty thing, isn't she?"

Paige had to admit she was a pretty horse, as horses went. And not as tall as Bright Star or as imposing as Jay's horse Thunder Boy.

"Come on in and get acquainted," he urged, his eyes pleading. "I'll be right here with you."

An anxious flutter in her stomach warned of oncoming panic. She said a quick prayer and stepped into the straw-covered stall.

"Good. Now say hello to Peaches."

"Hi." The word stuck in her throat.

Archie, the barn dog, chose that moment to enter Peaches's stall. The horse and dog touched noses and sniffed.

"They're friends," Paige said in surprise.

"Yeah. Archie is pretty much friends with all the horses."

Unable to resist, Paige reached down to pat Archie. "How are you doing, girl? Those puppies are getting big, aren't they?"

Peaches stuck her nose right by her hand, and Paige found herself petting the horse. "Is she doing this because she doesn't want Archie to get all the attention?"

"I'd say so. We kind of spoil her around here."

She smiled at that. It had never occurred to her a horse could be spoiled. Peaches assessed her with patient eyes, inviting Paige to continue petting her.

"Try stroking her along her neck," Jay suggested.

Paige did and felt Peaches's muscles ripple beneath her skin.

"You're doing fine," Jay said. "Are you feeling comfortable?"

She considered that for a moment and nodded. "I'm okay."

"Excellent. Would you like to brush her mane? She really likes that."

Paige's hand froze. Would it be just like brushing Krissy's hair when they were young? Both she and her sister had enjoyed those moments together.

"Okay, I'll try."

Jay handed her a stiff brush, which she pulled through Peaches's dusky-brown mane. The strands straightened to rest smoothly on the horse's sturdy neck. "Pretty girl," Paige crooned.

She was also increasingly aware of Jay's closeness. Although he wasn't touching her, she imagined she could feel the heat of his body. That if she leaned back, he'd wrap his strong arms around her. Hold her tight. Safe.

Somewhere in the barn, a phone rang. Automatically Paige stiffened, halting her wayward thoughts.

A few minutes later, Grandpa came from the house to talk to them. A deep frown creased his forehead.

"The school called. Bryan got into a fight while he was waiting for the bus to come home. He's being detained in the principal's office."

Paige's heart squeezed. "Was he hurt?"

"Didn't sound like it. But somebody will have to go pick him up."

"I'll go." She handed Jay the brush.

"I'm coming with you," he said, passing the brush to Grandpa.

Taking Paige's arm, he escorted her to his truck and helped her climb in.

When they were underway, she asked, "Does Bryan get into a lot of fights?" Being the guardian of a boy who often got into trouble wouldn't be easy.

"Don't think so. He's pretty easygoing and well liked by the other kids."

Paige could only wonder what had happened this afternoon to change that and if it had anything to do with Krissy's death.

Chapter Six

Bear Lake Grammar School, home of the Grizzlies according to the sign outside, was a one-story brick building about three blocks from the town's main street. There were still cars parked in the lot, presumably belonging to the teachers. Only a handful of students were hanging around in front of the school waiting to be picked up.

Paige hurried in through the double-door entrance, Jay right with her.

"Principal's office is on the left," he said.

She wheeled in that direction and pushed open the door without knocking. Sitting on a nearby chair, Bryan had his elbows on his thighs and his chin resting on his fists.

Paige knelt down in front of him. "Are you all right?"

He lifted his head. "I'm okay."

Leaning in closer, Jay lifted the boy's chin. "Looks like a cut lip. We ought to get some ice on that."

Bryan's gaze slid up to meet Jay's. A faint smile lifted his lips. "Other guy has a black eye."

Jay's reaction was to bump fists with Bryan, as though he condoned giving another boy a black eye.

Far more worried about her young charge's behavior, Paige asked, "Why were you fighting? Did the other boy start it?"

"Yeah, he did." His gaze slid away from hers.

"He hit you first?" Outraged, Paige looked around to see if the other boy was also being detained.

"Not exactly," Bryan admitted. "He sort of said something I didn't like."

"So you hit him?" She couldn't imagine why Bryan would strike out at someone just because he'd said something unpleasant. "Surely you know you were in the wrong to do that."

A woman in her mid-forties with brown hair graying at the temples stepped out of the office behind the counter. "I assume you're here for Bryan," she said. "I'm Mrs. Waterfield, the school principal."

Paige got to her feet and extended her hand. "I'm Bryan's aunt, Paige Barclay, his mother's sister. And this is Jay Red Elk, my grandfather's wrangler."

Jay acknowledged the principal with a nod.

"I was so sorry to hear about Bryan's mother having such a terrible accident," the principal said. "You have my condolences."

"Thank you. I'm sorry Bryan started a fight. I know he's upset about losing his mother, but—"

"As I understand the situation from Bryan," Mrs. Waterfield said, "the fight was about something the other boy said about you, Miss Barclay."

Paige's mouth dropped open. Her brows lowering into a frown, she turned to Bryan. "What in the world did the boy say?"

Bryan fidgeted, shuffling his feet back and forth. He didn't meet her eyes. "He'd heard about you trying to saddle Bright Star. He was making fun of you in front of all the guys."

"How in the world did he hear about that?" Paige couldn't imagine Jay had spread the word. Or Grandpa.

Bryan scrunched up his face. "He's Nathan's little brother."

She knelt again, placing her hand on his knee. "You hit the other boy because of me?"

"I guess." He glanced up at Jay. "People shouldn't laugh at stuff like that."

"You're right, son," Jay agreed in a tone that was both tender and loving. To Paige he said quietly, "I'll have a talk with Nathan later."

She nodded her thanks to Jay.

"Oh, Bryan…" A strange sense of joy filled Paige's chest and tightened her throat. Instinctively, she reached out to him, pulling him into an embrace. He'd been trying to *defend* her. However misguided the impulse might have been, she cherished the knowledge that he cared. "I'm so sorry you felt you had to hit him. It's never right to fight, you know."

"Yeah, well, you're my aunt and stuff."

"Yes, I am." Leaning back, she brushed his blond hair away from his forehead. "And I love you. But no more fighting, okay? Not about me or anything else."

His shrug was an acknowledgment of her words, but not a promise.

She struggled to her feet again. "May we take him home now, Mrs. Waterfield?"

"Of course, but I would like a moment to talk with you alone, if you have the time."

Jay got the hint. "Come on, buddy." He snared Bryan's arm. "We'll meet you out at the truck." As they went out the door, Jay slung his arm around the boy's shoulders.

Paige turned expectantly to Mrs. Waterfield. "Is there another problem?"

"No, not a problem." She clasped her hands in front of herself. "Bryan tells me you're to be his guardian and you'll be taking Bryan to Seattle. He'll be living there with you."

"Yes, that's the plan. My job is there and I own a small condo." Did the principal not approve? Was that what she had on her mind?

"I just wanted you to know we'll miss Bryan.

He's been a fine student and a leader. I hope he'll be happy living in Seattle."

Paige heard an echo of doubt in the principal's voice. "I'm hoping for that, too, Mrs. Waterfield. Very much so."

As Paige left the office, she wondered if the principal had intentionally tried to get her to question the decision she'd made. But what other choice did she have? Paige couldn't very well live here in Bear Lake. Her career was in the hospitality business. Not wrangling horses. Or working in a small-town diner or fast-food joint.

And that was about the only future a town like Bear Lake had to offer someone like her.

Krissy had to have known that when she appointed Paige as Bryan's guardian.

The next afternoon, while Bryan was still in school, Paige groomed Peaches under Jay's encouraging supervision.

"How'd you get into the hotel business?" he asked, handing her a brush for Peaches's mane.

Paige suspected the question was meant to take her mind off horses and onto something else. She supposed it was his way of being kind. Sweet of him, even if it didn't entirely work. But in fact she was mostly thinking about Jay and the easy way he had with horses. And wondering, if they weren't at odds over Bryan, if something more than merely being polite might develop.

"Growing up in Lewiston, I kept dreaming of visiting faraway places. I knew I'd never have enough money of my own to travel very far, so I decided to major in the hospitality business."

"Makes sense, I guess."

"Trust me, it does." Peaches turned her head to listen to the conversation. Idly, Paige petted her nose. "Particularly since I landed a job with Elite Hotels. They have properties all over England and Europe. I've already managed to visit a couple. It's wonderful to see the countryside and learn about different customs and cultures. Someday, with a lot of hard work, I'll be managing one of those hotels."

"That's a pretty ambitious goal. I've never felt the need to travel myself."

"Not everyone does." Jay seemed so content in his own skin. He knew his place in the world while Paige had struggled to find that sense of belonging that came so easily to him.

Which was one more reason she and Jay were so different. Just as she'd had different dreams than her own sister. And their parents.

Thursday afternoon, after she had finished brushing Peaches's coat, she led the horse out of her stall and into the corral. A mild case of nerves caused her hand to shake. But the horse followed her just like a well-trained dog on a leash. Except Peaches was much bigger.

Jay grinned at her as she walked the horse back into her stall. "You're looking like an old pro."

"I don't feel like one." She gave Peaches one quarter of an apple and unsnapped the lead rope.

"I think you'll be up on Peaches's back any day now."

She laughed, feeling good about her progress. "In your dreams, cowboy."

Friday morning, Jay, Grandpa and Paige all climbed in Jay's truck and left in time to be at Bryan's school at ten o'clock for Game Day. It was beautiful and sunny with only a cloud or two in the blue sky. A light breeze moved the tops of pine trees, making their needles shimmer. Days like this didn't often happen in Seattle, Paige mused.

Adults and children swarmed the playing field adjacent to the school. Babies in strollers and toddlers perched on their fathers' shoulders watched the passing crowd in fascination.

This was the kind of event Paige had so wished her parents had attended when she was in school. Now here she was with Jay acting as parents should, taking an interest in the their child's activities.

Except she and Jay weren't a couple, and she was doing her best to be a good guardian for Bryan.

On the field, chalked lines designated running

·aces, and a temporary stage had been set up for
he presentation of awards.

Standing on tiptoe, Paige tried to spot Bryan in
he crowd. "How will we know when Bryan is going
o race?"

"They'll announce the races over the loudspeak-
:rs," Grandpa said. He looked flushed with excite-
nent. Paige knew her cheeks were pink, too.

She did worry that Grandpa was breathing harder
han he should be after such a short walk.

"I wish we could see him. I want to make sure
le knows we're here." She remembered anxiously
searching the audience to find her parents when she
vas playing for the student musicals in high school.
More often than not, she was disappointed. She had
ried hard to understand her parents were busy with
he hardware store, but that did little to assuage the
etdown she always felt in their absence.

The hardware store was their life. And their live-
ihood, she admitted.

"There he is." Jay's shrill whistle nearly pierced
²aige's eardrums.

She looked where he was pointing, spotted Bryan
vaving and waved back to him. Once she and Brian
vere in Seattle, she vowed to attend every event
3ryan was in, no matter how inconvenient it might
·e for her. Then she remembered how annoyed her
·oss had been that she hadn't returned to Seattle
or the doctors' conference.

This is way more important, Mr. Armstrong.

The loudspeaker sputtered. A male voice announced, "Fifth grade boys. Line up for the forty-yard dash."

"That'll be Bryan's race," Grandpa said.

"Follow me." Using his size, Jay led them through the crowd to get closer to the starting line. Once there he stepped behind Paige and Grandpa to give them the best view.

"Good luck, Bryan!" she shouted.

He gave her a cute little grin then put on his determined face again.

There was lots of jostling on the starting line as more boys joined the group.

Acting as the starter, Mrs. Waterfield raised her starting gun. "Ready. Set. Go!" The gun went off and away the boys went.

Bryan had a good start, but he was neck and neck with another boy.

Jumping up and down, Paige's cheers mixed with Jay's big booming voice and those of the other parents in the crowd.

The race was over too fast. The crowd near the finish line cheered.

"Did he win?" Paige asked.

"Couldn't see," Jay answered, stepping out into the first lane and craning his neck to get a better look.

She went right with him. "We should've stood near the end."

But that hadn't been necessary. Bryan broke away from the gaggle of boys and trotted back to them with a big grin on his face. He held up one finger. "I told you I'd beat Toby this year."

"Way to go, kid." Jay gave him a big high five. So did Grandpa.

Paige started to do the same. Instead, she wrapped her arms around her nephew and hugged him tight. "Congratulations, Bryan. I'm so proud of you." For a moment, her eyes misted as she realized all that Krissy would miss not being here to watch her son grow up. *I'll take good care of him, Krissy. I promise.*

As the games went on, Bryan won the baseball toss but he ran out of steam on the longer race that took the runners all the way around the playing field. Toby won that one. Bryan didn't seem to mind too much.

The grand finale of the games was the tug-of-war between the fifth and sixth graders, boys and girls included.

Jay and Paige were maneuvering to find a good place to watch when she looked around for Grandpa. She'd lost track of him.

"What happened to Grandpa?" An uneasy feeling raised the hair on her nape.

"I don't know." Jay glanced over the crowd behind them. "He was right with us a minute ago."

"Maybe he felt like he was getting too much sun

and needed to find some shade." She looked toward the narrow ribbon of shadows the school building cast, but didn't see him. The temperature wasn't all that hot, maybe seventy degrees. Unlike Paige Grandpa was wearing a hat, as was Jay.

"I'll go look for him." Jay strode off toward the brick building.

Torn, Paige peered through the crowd. She'd really like to see the tug-of-war but was worried about Grandpa. For the moment, he'd have to be her priority. She jogged after Jay.

He checked the restroom while she stuck her head in the empty classroom nearest the playing field. He was sitting at one of the low desks, his head resting on the desktop.

"Are you all right?" Worry had her heart beating fast, and she sat down at the desk beside him.

He lifted his head. His face looked pale, his forehead beaded with sweat. "I'm fine, girl. Little too much excitement for these old bones is all."

"Are you sure?" He didn't look fine. Thinking he might be running a fever, she touched his forehead with the back of her hand. Despite the sweat he didn't seem too hot. "Do you need to go home? We can take you."

"The games aren't over, are they?"

Jay had come into the room. "Almost over. The tug-of-war is finishing up and then come the awards."

"Well, then…" Grandpa straightened. "You two better get out there to see Bryan get his medals. I'll wait here for you. The boy can show me when it's all over."

"I'll stay with you, Grandpa. Jay can—"

"No, you both go on. I'll rest here. I'll be raring to go in a few minutes."

Paige didn't like the idea of leaving him alone. She didn't like the way he was so pale yet sweating. Maybe she could get him in to see a doctor this afternoon. Over his strong objections, she imagined.

Just then a young woman she took to be a teacher stepped into the room. "Is everything all right here?"

Paige rested her hand on Grandpa's shoulder. "I think my grandfather may have gotten too much sun."

"That can definitely happen," the teacher said. "Let me get him some water." From a nearby cabinet, she produced a bottle of water. "Here you go."

"Thank you so much." Paige twisted the cap off and handed the bottle to her grandfather.

He took a long drink. "Now, you two go on. You want to see the boy get his medals."

Still reluctant, Paige hesitated.

The teacher said, "I'll keep an eye on him. Go ahead."

"Thank you."

"We won't be gone long, Henry." Jay gestured for

Paige to come with him. "You stay put and we'll be right back for you."

Relieved the teacher had agreed to stay with Grandpa, Paige followed Jay out of the classroom. "He looks sick to me. It may be something more than too much sun. I think I ought to stay."

"The teacher will watch out for him for few minutes. Henry gets extra tired these days when he has to stand for any length of time. That's why he sits to clean tack. I should've thought to bring a folding chair along today." He took her hand and hurried them toward the crowd waiting for the awards to be presented.

Even as she was tantalizingly aware of Jay's large hand wrapped around hers, Paige prayed that Grandpa was simply feeling his age. That the problem wasn't more serious.

They reached the front of the stage as the last of the awards were handed out by the principal.

Bryan hopped down from the platform and ran toward Jay and Paige, his medals swinging on red, white and blue ribbons around his neck.

"Hey, buddy, you did good." They high-fived.

Paige lifted the medals to get a better look. "If these were made out of real gold, you'd be a pretty rich kid." Filled with pride at his success, she ruffled his sweaty blond hair.

"Where's Grandpa?" Bryan asked.

"He's resting in one of the classrooms," Jay said. "He got too much sun. Let's go show him your medals."

The school bell rang, announcing lunchtime. Children hastily told their parents good-bye and raced for the cafeteria.

"Okay. But I gotta get my lunch soon. It's pizza day. I don't want 'em to run out."

"No problem. I'll race you." Jay took off, giving himself a head start.

"Hey, wait!" Bryan pounded after him.

Paige followed, worry about Grandpa hurrying her pace. Although, by the time she reached the celebration in the classroom, he seemed to have recovered. His color looked good, his enthusiasm high for Bryan's accomplishments.

Bryan didn't hang around long before he dashed out to buy his lunch.

As Paige rode back home in Jay's truck, she relived the morning, etching every exciting moment in her memory. *This is what it feels like to be a parent. She wouldn't have missed it for the world.*

Nor would she have missed the lingering warmth of Jay's hand as he held hers.

After lunch, Grandpa firmly refused to see a doctor. Instead he went to his room to take a nap. Despite her concern, Paige couldn't very well order him to be checked by a doctor.

So, with a sense of anticipation, Paige went out to the barn hoping for another horse grooming lesson from Jay.

To tamp down her bubbling excitement, she firmly reminded herself that in another week, after the guardianship hearing, she and Bryan would be in Seattle. She'd probably only see Jay once or twice a year, so there was no reason to expect more than a casual relationship during the remaining time she'd be in Bear Lake.

Inhaling the now familiar scents of horse, leather and hay, she walked to Peaches's stall and stopped abruptly. Her gaze skittered to Jay, who was saddling the horse. Disappointment took the fizz right out of her.

"I guess Peaches is going on a trail ride, huh?" Although she hadn't seen any would-be riders gathering at the corral and Nathan didn't seem to be around.

"Nope. No trail ride." Jay made sure the saddle was firmly in place. "I figure you're ready for a short stroll around the corral."

"On top of Peaches?" Her throat constricted.

His eyes sparkled with mischief. "Unless you'd prefer a piggyback ride."

No, she didn't think that was a good idea, for

far different reasons than her fear of getting on a horse—and falling off.

"I thought I'd still be grooming her," she protested.

"You already wield the brush like an old pro. Unless you want to spend the time learning to clean hooves."

She wrinkled her nose. That didn't sound like fun, and it meant she'd be within kicking distance of the horse.

He untied Peaches's lead rope. "Come on. I'll be right beside you the whole time. There's nothing to be afraid of." He led the horse out of her stall.

Paige stood frozen in place for a moment. She could go back to the house. Maybe find something to read. Or she could go for a walk. She still hadn't strolled up the dirt road to see where it led.

But without her permission, her feet followed Jay instead of running the other way. It was as if Krissy's boots had a mind of their own and were determined to return to their old life stuffed into a pair of stirrups.

Jay had the horse tied to a railing. "Come on, I'll boost you up."

He clasped his hands together. Grabbing the saddle horn, she placed her foot in his hands and up she went.

"Oh," she cried, clinging tightly to the horn for fear she'd slip off. Memories of her fall off the horse as a child sent chills down her back and made her leg ache.

"You okay?"

No! "It's so high up here."

Chuckling, he fussed with the stirrups. "Wait 'til I get you up on Thunder Boy."

She rolled her eyes. That was so not going to happen.

He checked to be sure the stirrups were the right length. "Now sit comfortably kind of back in the saddle. Squeeze your knees to hold on to the horse."

Use her knees? He had to be kidding. Her legs were bowed around Peaches's girth, only to have Paige's feet pointing in opposite directions, like an awkward plié; no way could she squeeze anything.

"Maybe Peaches needs to go on a diet," she muttered.

His mouth quirked into an amused smile as he handed her the reins. "I want you to hold the reins loosely in your left hand. You're not going to do anything with them this time. Just hold them."

"If I hold the reins, I'll have to let go of the saddle horn with that hand." That seemed like the most obvious thing in the world to her. And, at the moment, the most dangerous.

"Seems that way, doesn't it?"

She closed her free hand so tightly around the horn her knuckles turned white.

He untied the lead rope from the railing and patted Peaches on the nose. "I'm going to walk you around the corral now just like you walked her yesterday."

"Except I wasn't riding her then."

Jay stepped away from the railing. She rocked in the saddle with each step Peaches took. Paige closed her eyes. *I do not like this. No, I don't. I do not like this at all.* In her head, she sounded like the Grinch in the land of Who.

"You're doing great, Paige. Open your eyes. Enjoy the view."

She peeked. To her surprise they were halfway around the corral. The sun cast shadows from nearby trees, turning a part of the corral into a variegated pattern in shades of brown. She caught sight of the blue waters of Bear Lake down the hillside. But most of all, she saw Jay looking up at her. His rugged jaw relaxed into a smile. His eyes shone with encouragement.

Her heart did a tumble. Had anyone ever looked at her in quite that way? With approval? Pride? And something that seemed to be much more?

They reached the place where they had started.

"You want to go around again?" he asked.

She shook her head. "I think that's enough for today."

"You're sure? I'll let you steer if you want."

"Definitely not," she said with a laugh.

He looped the lead line over the railing. "Down you come then."

She swung her leg up over the horse's rump. His large hands closed around her waist, warm and strong, as he eased her to the ground. She turned to look up at him.

Their eyes met, and something electric sparked between them. Something that defied explanation. A snap. A connection.

"You were terrific." Slowly, he lowered his head.

When his lips touched hers, a shiver of yearning quickened her heartbeat, and her breath lodged in her lungs. Excitement churned through her midsection. Dreams she had never dared to dream raced through her head. The kiss didn't last long. The quick brush of his lips on hers was almost like a reward for a job well done. Even so, she continued to feel the imprint of his warmth. The sweetness of his kiss.

He took a step back, leaving her slightly unsteady on her feet.

"How about we go around twice tomorrow?" His voice sounded raspy, breathless.

She didn't know how to answer. It didn't matter. No matter how hard she might try, his kiss had left her unable to form a coherent thought.

Chapter Seven

Jay had no idea why he'd kissed Paige. He'd helped her off the horse. She'd felt so good right there in his arms. He'd been very proud of her courage. The way she'd swallowed her fears for one trip around the corral.

So he'd kissed her as if he'd had the right.

That one little kiss had rocked him all the way down to his boots.

Dumb idea, Red Elk. She wasn't going to stick around. He might've gotten her on a horse once, but it wasn't like she'd be joining a Western mounted troupe and parade in a Fourth of July rodeo anytime soon.

Hours later, as he walked through the stable doing his last check of the horses for the night, he could still taste her sweet lips. Feel her slender figure in his arms. Smell the honeysuckle scent of her shampoo.

He and Bryan were taking a dozen riders on an all-day trail ride to Mount Thompson in the morning. He'd be well away from Paige. He'd forget about her lips and how he'd like to kiss her again.

That was the smart thing to do.

As he returned to his quarters, he glanced toward the house. The light was on in the room where Paige slept. He wondered what she was doing. If she was thinking about their kiss.

She'd looked as stunned as he had felt when they broke the kiss. She hadn't slapped him or seemed mad. For the longest time, neither of them had said a word.

Then Jay had led Peaches into her stall and unsaddled her. Standing silently in the middle of the barn, Paige had watched him.

"Bryan will be home soon," she finally said, her whisper like the rustle of leaves on the ground blown along by a gentle breeze.

He'd nodded, and she'd left the stable, leaving Jay wondering when he'd turned into a mute. He hadn't been much more talkative at dinner, which worked out okay because Bryan kept yammering about Game Day and the race and baseball toss he'd won.

Jay kicked the gravel on the walkway between the house and his quarters. He'd get a good night's sleep and be on the trail early in the morning.

That's what he did for a living. That's who he

was. Not some guy sitting at a desk in a downtown high-rise wearing a suit.

Not a man who got a second look from a woman like Paige.

First thing in the morning, Paige heard from Mr. Armstrong. The medical conference coordinator insisted he had arranged for a full breakfast for the attendees. Paige assured her boss that wasn't the case and emailed him the signed copy of the contract.

An hour later, Armstrong's secretary called to say they couldn't get the PowerPoint projector to work. Granted, the machine was sometimes temperamental, but how was Paige supposed to fix it from five hundred miles away? Someone, namely her assistant, should have checked it out yesterday before the conference started.

Guilt tweaked her conscience. If she had returned to Seattle when she'd planned, she would have taken care of that detail.

But seeing Bryan's excitement at Game Day was too special to have missed. And there was no sense to go streaking to Seattle at this late hour. She'd no more than arrive and she'd have to return to Bear Lake.

With Jay and Bryan on an all-day trail ride, and Nathan and Grandpa leading a group of riders on a two-hour trek, Paige found herself all alone in the quiet house.

She hadn't wanted Grandpa to go given his health. He waved off her concern, saying, "I've been riding horses since I was two. Not about to stop now."

She really wished he'd see a doctor for a checkup.

Feeling at loose ends, she wandered outside. With most of the horses gone, only the breeze in the treetops and periodic bird calls interrupted the silence. Somewhere there was a woodpecker busily at work tap-tap-tapping. The faint sound of a motorboat on the lake barely reached her.

Archie trotted out of the barn, her feathery tail wagging. Her pregnancy seemed to make her belly grow every day, and Paige felt a twinge of envy. What would it be like to carry a child inside her? Jay's child.

She felt a rush of warmth flush her body, and firmly quashed that sensation.

She knelt to pet the dog. "Are you lonely, too? Bet you wish you'd gone with Bryan."

Lifting her head, Archie licked her face. Giggling at the sensation, she recalled pleading with her parents to get her a puppy. Her mother had made it quite clear there was rarely anyone at home to take care of an animal, and there was no way she was going to clean up his messes after a long day at the hardware store.

Paige hadn't bothered to ask again.

With a resigned sigh, she walked toward the stables. Archie stayed right at her side.

"You'll let me know if there's a bear around, won't you?"

Archie didn't comment, but Paige was pretty sure she'd sound the alert if she spied a big black bear lumbering through the neighborhood.

However, Archie did seem to be guiding her. When she started to turn into the barn Archie stepped in front of her, all but forcing her to change direction and head for the stables.

She laughed. Archie's border collie genes were showing. Apparently Paige was the only creature around she could herd.

To her surprise, she discovered Peaches and one other horse still in their stalls. While she had been helping Bryan clean tack, she had overheard Grandpa and Nathan talking about the other horse having a gimpy leg. They were going to rest him for a few days.

Peaches nickered and hung her head over the side of the stall.

"Hi, girl." Paige rubbed the horse's velvet nose. "How come they left you behind? Weren't there any inexperienced riders today? Bet you and Archie both hate to miss out on all the fun." Although Paige was sure she'd find a full day's ride excruciatingly painful and punctuated by moments of terror.

As though Archie had done her duty delivering Paige to the stables, she went into Peaches's stall and curled up in the corner.

Feeling particularly courageous, Paige found the grooming brush. With only the slightest nervous twinge, she entered the stall and began brushing Peaches's dusky-brown mane.

"You do like attention, don't you?" She kept brushing and stroking the horse. Peaches seemed to be enjoying Paige's efforts and, to her surprise, Paige was, too.

After a few minutes, she had a totally outlandish thought. No one was around to see her making a fool of herself. If she could manage to saddle Peaches, she might be able to mount her and ride her around the corral a time or two. She had watched both Jay and Bryan saddle a horse. Nathan, too.

Now that she thought about it, putting a saddle on the back of a horse didn't seem so hard. Or scary. Not when the horse was Peaches, anyway.

In the tack room, she found Peaches's saddle and blanket. She carried them back to her stall.

Okay, Lord, I'm going to need a little help here.

Drawing in a deep breath to build up her courage, she held the blanket out in front of her and stepped up to the horse.

"Now, Peaches, you have to be extra patient with me." When she placed the blanket on Peaches's back, the horse didn't seem at all disturbed. "Good girl. I'll get the hang of this yet."

Hefting the saddle was a different matter. She'd

forgotten to hook up the stirrups to get them out of the way.

She tried again. This time she got the saddle settled. Facing the right way! She cinched the saddle into place and stood back to admire her work.

"Not so bad for a city girl, huh?"

Peaches nodded. Archie stood and stretched. It looked as though she was ready to go for a run.

After another moment appraising her success, she realized something was missing. Something important.

The bridle and reins.

Checking her watch, she found the trail ride wasn't due back for nearly an hour. If she could figure out how to get the bridle over the horse's head and the bit in her mouth, she'd still have time to go once around the corral all by herself.

What do you think about that, cowboy?

Fortunately, the tack for each horse was kept together. Even more fortunate, Peaches sensed Paige's inexperience and practically put the bit in her own mouth. Or maybe it was the Lord who was giving her a helping hand.

She led Peaches into the corral. Using a big rock to stand on, Paige leveraged herself onto the saddle.

"Sweetheart," she crooned, patting the animal's neck. "You are the best horse in the entire world."

The way Archie was watching, her head tilted

to one side, Paige didn't think she was all that impressed with her horsemanship.

The reins in one hand, the saddle horn grasped by the other, Paige gave Peaches a little nudge with her heels. To her great delight, the horse started forward. If she'd been wearing a cowboy hat—and had a free hand—she would have waved it in the air. *Ride 'em, cowgirl!*

With Peaches's cooperation, she took one turn around the corral. That went so well, she decided to try another one.

She wasn't sure how much time had passed when she sensed someone approaching the outfitting station. She turned in her saddle and saw Bryan walking toward her on the road leading a big gray horse that was limping.

"Aunt Paige! What are you doing?" he shouted.

Heat raced to her cheeks. Peaches decided on her own to trot over to meet Bryan by the fence. Paige gripped the saddle horn with all her strength as she bounced up and down, her feet coming out of the stirrups.

Peaches stopped abruptly.

Paige barely managed to hold her seat.

"I'm riding Peaches," she gasped. "What does it look like?"

A big grin creased his face. "Looks like you're not as scared as you used to be."

Paige took that as the finest compliment she'd ever received.

Now all she had to do was get off Peaches without breaking her neck. She dismounted with about as much grace as an ungainly kid belly flopping into a swimming pool.

It took her a minute to regain her breath. "So why are you back so early?"

"Sir Grayson threw a shoe. Jay had me trade horses with the guy who was riding him. I had to walk Grayson back home." Bryan led the horse into the corral. "Jay said I should call the farrier, tell him we need a horse shod."

Using the reins, Paige walked Peaches toward her stall.

"Jay and Grandpa will hoot when I tell 'em that you've been riding Peaches all by yourself," Bryan said.

Paige grimaced. She didn't want them laughing at her again. "It probably isn't necessary to mention that, honey. It could be our little secret."

Bryan glanced over his shoulder and grinned. "Nah, that's too good a secret to keep."

Tattletale!

Jay had his trail riders back to the stable by four o'clock. With the exception of Sir Grayson throwing a shoe, the ride had gone fine. Thanks to the riders who'd had some experience.

Bryan came out of the barn to help unsaddle and water the horses. "Guess what Aunt Paige was doing when I got here with Grayson?"

"I can't imagine." *Probably packing to get back to Seattle as quickly as she could to avoid having him kiss her again.* He lifted the saddle off Thunder Boy.

"She was riding Peaches!" He giggled and grinned.

Jay nearly dropped the saddle. "All alone?"

"Yeah. She nearly fell off when I showed up, but she was sitting in the saddle."

"Who saddled the horse for her?"

Bryan shrugged. "Dunno. Guess she did it herself. Nathan and Grandpa weren't back yet. They are now though."

Surprised as a grasshopper about to get stepped on, Jay smiled to himself. That was worth a celebration.

Nathan came out of the barn to help with the horses. "What's so funny?"

Bryan told him.

"Whoa!" Nathan said. "That's awesome. Maybe she's more like Krissy that we thought."

Jay didn't think so. Krissy never feared a thing. Paige had to overcome her fears. That took a whole lot more spirit and mental strength.

After they got the horses cooled down, fed and put away, Jay went over to the main house. He heard the piano playing as he walked into the mudroom and hung his hat on a peg. The music sounded familiar, but he couldn't name the tune.

He strolled as far as the door to the living room. Henry was dozing in his chair, so Jay leaned against the doorjamb to watch Paige play. She had pretty hands. Slender fingers. Graceful. Yet the music she was making was strong and confident.

She was that way on the inside, too. Strong. Confident. Willing to confront her fears. A pretty incredible combination.

She tapped the closing notes of the piece, then rested her hands in her lap.

"Very nice." Jay walked into the room.

She turned and scowled. "You're doing your sneaking-up-on-people thing again."

"Nope. You were concentrating so hard, you just didn't hear me."

"Whatever." She swiveled around on the piano bench.

"I hear we have something to celebrate," he said.

Henry opened his eyes. "What's that?"

"Miss Paige Barclay saddled and rode Peaches all on her own today."

Color flooded her cheeks. "Bryan doesn't know how to keep a secret."

"You really rode her?" Henry asked. "By yourself?"

"Really, it's not like I climbed Mount Everest. You all ride horses every day."

"Yeah, but you were scared spitless the other day." Jay hooked his thumbs in his jean pockets and rocked back on his heels.

"I'm proud of you, girl," Henry said. "I know you've never liked horses, but we'll make a wrangler out of you yet."

Shaking her head, she stood. "That is so not going to happen, Grandpa."

"Maybe not," Jay said. "But I think we ought to celebrate your first solo ride. How 'bout you, Henry?"

"A celebration does seem to be in order."

"Great. Then let's all go out to dinner at the Pine Tree Diner." He turned to Paige. "They've got great steaks. Buffalo burgers served with a pile of skinny fries. Barbecued ribs. What do you say? Saturday night family dinner out?"

"I, um…" Her cheeks glowed pink again. "Sure. It's got to be better than my cooking. If Grandpa feels up to it. You looked pretty tired when you came back from the trail ride."

"I'm fine, girl. Not going to turn down a juicy steak when Jay's paying."

"You got it, old man," Jay said with a laugh. "I'll go round up Bryan and get myself cleaned up. Say a half hour?"

Paige nodded, and Jay left the house, his footsteps

lighter than when he'd arrived. He had to remind himself this wasn't like a real date. It was *family*.

He liked that thought, too.

Paige and Bryan sat in the backseat of Jay's extended cab pickup, Grandpa in the front with Jay. The sensation of being a family, of all going out to dinner together, encompassed Paige like a warm, cozy blanket. Yet this wasn't reality. All too soon she would take Bryan to Seattle. It would be just the two of them.

To shake off the thought, she turned away to look out the truck window. The sun cast lengthening shadows as it headed toward sunset, and when they passed the municipal park, Paige caught a glimpse of Bear Lake. Streaks of gold shimmered across the rippling surface as boats cut through the water.

"Do you like to go boating?" she asked Bryan.

"It's okay, I guess."

"We've got lots of boating around Seattle. I've got some friends that can take us out on the Sound. We could even try to catch some fish."

His half lift of one shoulder indicated little interest in her suggestion. She'd have to check online to see what sort of activities were available near her condo for a boy Bryan's age. Otherwise it would be a long, lonely summer for him.

Jay pulled the truck into a parking spot in front

of the Pine Tree Diner, a three-story pink building with white trim. A sign on the front window indicated they served authentic Czech dishes, which sounded more interesting than ordinary diner fare.

Paige climbed out of the pickup, an awkward maneuver in a skirt and heels.

Jay held open the restaurant door, and they all filed inside. A pleasant murmur of conversation met them along with the scent of fresh coffee and burgers on the grill.

An attractive blonde wearing a neat white blouse and slacks stepped out from behind the cash register with a handful of menus. Her welcoming smile greeted them.

"Hello, Henry." She winked at Bryan. "Good to see you, Jay. You haven't been around for a while."

"Hey, Alisa." He removed his hat. "How's the new bride doing?"

A blush tinted her cheeks. "Couldn't be better. Nick's a dream, and Mama couldn't be happier having a chef around to share the workload."

"I bet." He chuckled and turned to Paige. "This is Krissy's sister from Seattle, Paige Barclay. She's been staying with Henry for a few days. This is Alisa Machak, owner of—"

"Alisa *Carbini*," the young woman corrected with a smile.

"Yeah, that's going to take some getting used to."

Alisa's expression turned somber as she greeted

Paige. "I'm so sorry about your sister. I'd wanted to get to Krissy's funeral service, but—" Her lips slanted into an expression of apology. "When we're shorthanded, it's hard to get away."

"Please don't worry about it." The memory of the funeral tightened Paige's chest. "Pastor Walker performed a very nice service for her. I'm sure Krissy would have been pleased." That little white lie pained Paige. She had no idea what her sister's feelings were about church, only that she rarely, if ever, attended.

"Now then…" Alisa glanced around at the booths that were covered in bright pink vinyl, most of which were occupied. "Do you want to be seated inside or out on the patio?"

"Let's sit outside," Grandpa said. "Maybe we'll catch the sunset."

"You okay with that?" Jay asked Paige.

"That'll be fine."

Alisa hooked her arm around Bryan's shoulders. "Come on, buddy. I heard you blew everybody away at Game Day yesterday."

"Yeah, I did." The boy fell into step with Alisa, relating the details of his grand success.

A twinge of envy pricked Paige as she saw the easy way Alisa interacted with Bryan. Would he ever be that comfortable with her?

The rest of them followed Alisa out onto a lovely patio where tables were set up around a big fire pit, although there was no fire at the moment. A mountain range to the west was caught in the slanting rays of sunlight casting the dips and valleys in shadow.

After seating them, Alisa gave them menus and took their drink orders. "Your waitress will be right with you."

When she left, Paige asked, "Is she really a newlywed?"

Grandpa flipped open his menu. "Yep, got married just a few weeks ago."

"They had the reception in the banquet room here at the diner," Jay said. "You should've seen the layout. Every Czech dish you can imagine. Real goulash and sauerkraut—"

"That tasted gross." Bryan wrinkled his nose.

"You sure liked the apple strudel, young man," Grandpa said. "You had three helpings. With ice cream."

"Yeah, well, I was hungry."

Grandpa nudged him with his elbow. "Glad you found something to eat or you would have starved, right?"

Bryan ducked his head. "Yeah, maybe."

"Kid's always hungry," Jay said. "I caught him once eating a handful of the oats we feed the horses."

Bryan scowled at him. "Only one bite! I wanted to see if it tasted like oatmeal."

"Did it?" Paige asked, curious.

"Naw. It was like cardboard. I don't know how they eat that stuff."

They all laughed, and Paige sat back, enjoying the lighthearted teasing between Grandpa and Bryan, and the way Jay jumped right in as though he was family, too.

With Jay sitting next to her, his arm brushing hers from time to time, the scent of his aftershave teasing her senses, she felt a part of the family, as well. He had a deep, masculine laugh that reached inside her, creating an unfamiliar fluttery feeling. The fact that they were *celebrating* her first solo ride on Peaches tickled her funny bone. She couldn't stop smiling.

As she listened to their banter, she realized dinner conversation had almost been entirely absent in her family. Except when there was something about the hardware store that needed to be discussed. Or when Krissy was in trouble.

She almost envied the years Krissy had lived with Grandpa, particularly while Grandma Lisbeth was still alive.

Glancing around at the other diners, she noted they were mostly moms and dads with children, all of who were laughing and having a good time. She didn't begrudge them their happiness. But her own sense of loneliness, of the lack of deep friendships and a loving family, welled up in her chest.

She quickly repressed the feeling. She and Bryan would be a family. Just the two of them. She vowed they'd be happy together. Bryan might be her only chance to ever be, if not a mother, a woman who had a child to raise and love. At least for a few years.

When the waitress returned, Grandpa asked for a medium-rare steak, Jay ordered a buffalo burger and Bryan had a regular hamburger. Paige splurged, ordering sliced veal in a cream sauce with mashed potatoes and fresh string beans.

As they waited for their dinners, the conversation turned to business and the Bear Lake Outfitters' website.

"You have a website, Grandpa?" Paige hadn't known that or she would have checked it out.

Grandpa nodded. "Yep. Krissy set us up with one and taught me how to keep track of things. We get most of our business from the web these days."

Beyond surprised, Paige said, "I didn't know Krissy knew anything about computers."

"She was a smart girl, all right. When she wanted to be."

"Mom always said I got my smarts from her," Bryan said. "That's how come I get good grades." A sense of pride and love rode on the way Bryan sat a little straighter and puffed out his chest.

Paige wanted to reach out and hug him. "I'm sure you got a lot of good things from your mother, honey."

Their dinner arrived, and they ate in silence for a time. Paige's veal was melt-in-your-mouth tender, the sauce delicious and the mashed potatoes were the creamiest she'd ever tasted. The beans crunched when she bit into them. Elite Hotels would do well to hire the chef from Pine Tree Diner. Although that seemed unlikely since he was apparently married to the owner.

Paige was too stuffed to finish all of her meal, but her three male escorts devoured theirs and ordered fresh apple pie à la mode. Paige had no idea how they could hold that much food.

As they finished the ice cream, Paige noticed Grandpa pressing his hand to his chest. Sweat beaded his forehead. His color had gone gray.

"Grandpa, are you all right?" She started to get to her feet.

"Ate too much." He pushed back his chair, stood unsteadily for a moment, then crumpled to the ground.

"Grandpa!" she cried.

Both she and Jay reached Grandpa at the same time. Jay pressed his fingers to Grandpa's neck to check his pulse.

"He's still alive." Jay met Paige's eyes for an instant, telegraphing his concern. Then he snatched his cell phone from his pocket and called 9-1-1.

Please, Lord... She left her prayer unfinished, knowing God would understand her plea.

Chapter Eight

Jay followed the ambulance in his truck, Bryan riding with him. Paige rode with Henry and the EMTs.

"Is Grandpa going to die?" Bryan's voice sounded choked with tears he was trying not to shed.

Jay glanced at him. Ever since Henry had collapsed, the kid had been as pale as a rabbit in its winter coat. A pretty scary thing for a youngster of twelve to see.

It was pretty scary for Jay, too. He didn't want to consider what would happen if the old guy passed away. That would be tough on Bryan. And Paige. Losing two family members in less than two weeks would be hard to face.

"I don't know," he said with honesty. "We'll find out after the doctors get a look at him."

"First thing the ambulance guy did was put an oxygen mask on Grandpa." His chin trembled.

"That's a good sign." Jay tried to reassure Bryan

when, in fact, he was more worried about Henry's rapid pulse. It had felt like Henry's heart was trying to launch itself out of his chest. "It means your grandfather was still breathing. He just needed a little help getting enough oxygen."

Bryan didn't seem entirely satisfied with Jay's answer.

Siren screaming and emergency lights flashing, the ambulance cleared a path down the highway. Jay hung close behind it. He remembered how he had raced Annie to the hospital when she started to bleed rather than wait for an ambulance, and a knot formed in his gut.

They hadn't been able to save her at the hospital.

He prayed to God that Henry would make it.

The ambulance turned onto a side street, slowing only as it reached the emergency entrance to Bear Lake Medical Clinic. A modern two-story building, it served the needs of residents and tourists in a fifty-mile radius.

Jay peeled into the parking lot and found a spot near the main entrance.

He and Bryan walked in through the automatic doors. Jay headed for the information desk. A middle-aged woman wearing a blue volunteer jacket looked up expectantly.

"The ambulance is bringing Henry Stephenson into the emergency room now. Is there any way we can get in there to see him?"

"Are you a relative?"

Jay hooked his arm around Bryan's shoulder. "He's Stephenson's great-grandson."

She nodded, glanced at Bryan with sympathetic eyes then clicked a few keys on her computer. "We don't have him checked into the system yet. It will be better if you wait here in the lobby until they have him settled. It can get pretty chaotic in there I'll let you know when it's all right to go in."

"Okay." At least Paige was there with Henry She'd see to it that Henry got the attention he needed.

Jay looked around. An assortment of chairs were arranged facing a television set that was showing a basketball play-off game with the sound muted Two couples were staring at the screen. A mother sat rocking a baby in her arms.

"Let's find ourselves a couple seats, son. This may be a long wait."

Bryan scrubbed his eyes with the back of his hands. His shoulders slack, he found himself a chair and plopped himself down.

Jay sat next to him, looped his arm around the boy and gave his shoulder a squeeze. After losing his mother so recently, the wait was going to seem longer to Bryan than it was to Jay.

He wondered how Paige was holding up. She didn't seem the type to get hysterical. Which would be good if Henry got himself all riled up.

Lifting his arm from around Bryan, Jay leaned forward and rested his forearms on his thighs. He lowered his head and closed his eyes. *Lord, if You can see Your way clear to keeping Henry here on Earth for a while longer, I sure would appreciate it. So would a lot of other good people like Bryan and Paige.*

"There's nothing wrong with me!" Grandpa had continually fussed at Dr. Johansen since he had arrived in the emergency room. Despite the oxygen he was getting through his nose, when he drew a deep breath, it wheezed through his chest. Sweat continued to bead his forehead.

Holding his hand, Paige tried to calm her grandfather and not let him see how scared she was. "Let the doctor listen to your heart, Grandpa. He needs to be sure you're all right."

"I got a little dizzy. Happens to everybody sometimes."

The doctor cranked up the bed so Grandpa was in a more seated position instead of lying flat on his back. "Getting dizzy only happens to me when I stand on my head too long. Is that what you did, Henry?" The doctor had Henry lean forward so he could put his stethoscope on his back.

"Bah. Your pricking and prodding at me isn't going to help. I'll be fine once I get home."

The doctor straightened. "I enjoy your company

so much, Henry, I think we'll just keep you around for a while. First thing, I'm going to get the portable X-ray machine in here so we can figure out what's going on in your chest."

"Same thing that's always been going on in there, youngster. What do you expect?" Grandpa groused.

"Behave yourself, Grandpa." Paige squeezed his hand.

His scowl deepened the lines across his forehead into crevasses.

"The nurse will be here in a minute to take some blood," the doctor said. "Then we'll get that picture of your chest."

"Waste of your time and my money," Grandpa complained.

The doctor stepped out of the curtained cubicle. Paige admonished her grandfather to rest quietly until she returned, then went after the doctor. She had to agree that Dr. Johansen seemed quite young, his boyish face and blond hair giving him a youthful appearance. But she had no reason to doubt his experience or skill.

"Doctor, do you have any idea yet what's wrong with my grandfather?"

He looked up from the notes he was writing on a chart. "I can't be sure of the seriousness of his problem until we get some test results back, but at this point it looks like pulmonary edema."

Paige felt the blood drain from her face. "That doesn't sound good."

"It's fortunate you got him to the clinic as quickly as you did. If his heart is causing the edema, then it could be very serious."

Her own heart plummeted to her stomach. "Is he—"

"Assuming I don't find a heart condition that requires surgery, I think we'll be able to stabilize him within a day or two. Then medication should prevent a further crisis. He's a tough ol' guy." The doctor smiled, trying to reassure her. "I imagine he's passed down some pretty strong genes."

Paige wasn't so sure about that.

A nurse wearing blue scrubs went into the cubicle.

"Thank you, Doctor," Paige said. She followed the nurse in an effort to protect her from the worst of Grandpa's disagreeable disposition.

A few minutes later when the X-ray technician arrived, he asked her to step outside the cubicle. That seemed like a good time for Paige to find Jay and bring him and Bryan up-to-date.

The moment she entered the lobby, Jay was on his feet. His dark brows lowered, reflecting her own concern for Grandpa. She was enormously grateful Jay was there. That she didn't have to go through this alone. That she had someone to lean on. For most of her life, she hadn't had anyone to lean on except herself.

Bryan turned in his chair and looked up at her. His chin trembled.

Paige leaned down to kiss him on the top of his head.

"Can the doctor fix Grandpa?" he asked.

"Yes, honey, Grandpa is going to be fine." She glanced up at Jay. "They're doing a chest X-ray now and there will probably be more tests. The doctor thinks he has pulmonary edema."

Jay's Adam's apple bobbed, and he looked away.

Sitting up on his knees, Bryan held on to the back of his chair. "What's pulmonary whatever you said?"

"I'm not quite sure. I think it has something to do with Grandpa not being able to breathe well." Several times since she'd arrived in Bear Lake, Paige had noticed him gasping for air. She should have forced him to see a doctor then, not wait until it was an emergency. Regret for her failure to take action weighed on her conscience.

"I should've known there was something wrong," Jay said. "He's so stubborn." He jammed his fingertips in his hip pockets. "He kept saying it was just old age. I believed him."

"You're not a doctor, Jay. You couldn't know." Yet she blamed herself. Ever the *good* daughter.

The nurse who had drawn Grandpa's blood came

out of the emergency room. She crossed the lobby to Paige.

"They're going to take your grandfather downstairs for an electrocardiograph and an ultrasound," the woman told Paige. "After that, they'll admit him to the hospital and take him to a room upstairs."

"Will we be able to see him then?" Paige asked.

"Of course." The nurse glanced at Bryan. "It may take a while."

"We'll wait," Jay said.

"Maybe you should take Bryan home," Paige suggested. "It's already late."

Bryan lowered his brows. "I wanna stay, too. I'm not a baby."

"No, you're not," Paige agreed, realizing it was important to Bryan to be treated as an adult when he was so worried about Grandpa.

As she was about to leave, the nurse said, "We have a small chapel just opposite the gift shop." She gestured toward the rear of the lobby. "It's always quiet there. The pews are quite comfortable. I can tell reception where you'll be."

Paige thanked the nurse, who then vanished back into the emergency room.

In unspoken agreement, Paige, Jay and Bryan headed for the chapel, a small, intimate room with three short wooden pews on each side separated by a center aisle. Soft music played in the background as they sat down, the cushioned pews as comfortable as the nurse had promised. Paige studied the mural across the front of the chapel—a tranquil scene featuring a quiet valley cut by a winding, placid river and surrounded by soaring mountains covered with stately trees.

"That's beautiful," she said.

Jay rested his arm across the pew behind her. "It's the river that flows into Bear Lake from the north. It's not far from Henry's place."

"Someday I'd like to see it in person."

"I'll take you."

His offer sent a curl of pleasure through Paige. Sighing, she repressed the feeling and tried to ease the tension in her shoulders.

"Here, let me. Lean forward." Jay's hands closed over her shoulders. His thumbs gently worked her knotted muscles, circling them, easing the tightness.

She almost groaned aloud relishing his touch. If she could bottle the sensation, she'd take it back to Seattle with her and pull it out on those days when one too many crises at the hotel plagued her.

Except Jay wouldn't really be there massaging her stress away, only her memory of this one time.

Slouched on the pew next to Jay, Bryan said, "Are we supposed to pray or something?"

Guilt flushing her cheeks, Paige quickly straightened. "Would you like to?"

"I guess."

"Okay. Why don't we all hold hands and you can

say a prayer for Grandpa." She grasped Jay's hand and reached in front of him to take Bryan's. She bowed her head. "You go ahead and start whenever you're ready."

"Dear God." He paused and cleared his throat. "I love Grandpa a lot and I don't want him to die. I know he's old and maybe You want him up there with You to take care of Your horses or somethin'. But I'd sure like it if You could leave him here with me for a while." He sniffed. "Please, God. Amen."

"Amen," Paige echoed, tears stinging her eyes.

Jay's "Amen" followed hers, a deep sound that was more a vibration in his chest than a spoken word.

An hour or so later, Dr. Johansen arrived in the chapel. Paige, Jay and Bryan, who had been dozing, gathered around him.

"I've sedated Mr. Stephenson, and he's resting comfortably in his room now." The doctor's white jacket looked wrinkled and his eyes seemed tired.

"What did the tests tell you?" Paige asked.

"Definitely pulmonary edema, but I can't be definitive yet about the heart's involvement. We'll do some more tests in the morning. Meanwhile, I've ordered medication for his high blood pressure and a diuretic to reduce the buildup of fluid around his heart."

Paige imagined Grandpa would hate taking the pills. He'd always refused to admit any weakness.

"When can Grandpa come home?" Bryan asked.

"If all goes well, I'd say a couple days." The doctor's smile softened as he answered Bryan. "Guess you're going to miss him, huh?"

"Yes, sir. He's a real good grandpa."

"I'm sure he is," the doctor said.

"Can we go see him?" Bryan asked.

Recognizing the boy's distress, Paige rested her hand on his shoulder. "He's sleeping now. We can come back to see him tomorrow."

The faint sound of a siren penetrated the quiet of the chapel. Dr. Johansen checked his pager. "I think it would be fine if you went up to your grandpa's room for just a minute. If you'll excuse me."

"Of course, Doctor," Paige said. The poor man was having a busy night in the emergency room.

Jay got Grandpa's room number from the receptionist, and they walked up the stairs to the second floor. As the doctor had indicated, Grandpa was asleep. He was still getting extra oxygen and he'd been hooked up to a heart monitor. The green line tracked across the screen, the rhythmic heartbeat reassuring.

"I can see his chest going up and down," Bryan whispered. "That means he's breathing, right?"

Jay pointed to the monitor. "That bouncing line

says his heart's beating, too. Your grandpa is doing fine, son."

Paige wished she could be as confident as Jay about Grandpa's health. At the age of eighty-five, any heart condition could put him in a perilous situation.

Who would take care of Grandpa if he became incapacitated?

An ache in her chest bloomed. If Krissy hadn't been so reckless, she would have been here to help their grandfather.

Now only Paige was left. How would she ever manage to care for both Bryan and Grandpa?

Like a crystal glass shattering, she envisioned her dreams and career splintering into a thousand pieces.

Thy will be done, Lord. Thy will, not mine.

Her prayer lanced her heart like a shard of glass.

Midmorning the next day Jay drove Paige and Bryan back to the hospital. He'd spent a restless night worrying about Henry. From the smudges beneath Paige's eyes, he guessed she hadn't slept well, either.

They found Henry sitting up in bed, feeling better and complaining loudly. "Do you know what they brought me for breakfast? Hog slop, that's what. For what I'm going to have to pay, I ought to get a whole raft of bacon and eggs."

"That wouldn't be good for your heart, Grandpa."

Paige leaned over to kiss him on the forehead. She was trying to calm the ol' guy down, but it wasn't working. He went on a tear about the needles they had stuck in him and the way his hospital gown didn't give him a "lick of privacy."

Jay couldn't blame him for complaining. He didn't like being in a hospital any more than Henry did. Fortunately his only hospital stay had been due to a broken leg he'd suffered in a bronc riding contest. He hoped to keep it that way for a long time to come.

When Henry was wheeled out of his room for yet another test, Jay and the others took their leave.

Once home, Jay was relieved to be back with his horses and the quiet of the mountains.

It wasn't long before Bryan sought him out in the stable.

"Can I talk to you?" His brows were drawn so low they almost hid his light brown eyes.

Jay scooped a serving of oats into Thunder Boy's feed bag. "Sure, kid. What did you want to talk about?" From the boy's expression, it was something serious.

"It's about Aunt Paige and her being my guardian 'n' stuff."

"Okay." Jay leaned one arm on the stall partition. "I thought you'd been getting along pretty good with Paige lately."

"She's okay, I guess." He rubbed Thunder Boy's nose. "For a girl, anyway."

"Yeah, I think so, too." Probably more than he should.

Bryan's jaw tightened. "I don't want to go live with her in Seattle."

"I understand, but—"

"No, you don't! Grandpa's sick and he's gonna need me to take care of him. If I don't watch out for him, he could die. I gotta be here in case he has a heart attack or collapses again."

Jay dropped the feed scoop back into the sack of oats. He framed Bryan's face between his hands so the boy would look him in the eye. "The doctor's going to give him some medicine so that won't happen. By the time we bring him home from the hospital, he'll be feeling like his old self. You'll see." Jay prayed his words weren't a lie. At eighty-five there were no guarantees.

"You can't be sure of that." His chin puckered. "You gotta stop Aunt Paige. Make her see that it would be better if I stayed here with Grandpa and you. Grandpa will need me. I know he will."

Pulling the youngster into his arms, Jay racked his brain for an alternative. Henry would likely need help sooner rather than later. He could hire a caregiver, but that would fry Henry's beans to have some stranger fussing over him all day and night.

Jay would be more than willing to do what he

could for Henry. But someone had to run the out-fitting business, handle the trail rides and overnight excursions. Nathan wasn't ready to take on that job on his own.

"Please, Jay. Talk to the judge." The boy sobbed, his voice muffled against Jay's chest. "Tell him I can stay with you. That you'll be my guardian."

"I don't know how—"

Bryan pushed away from Jay. His eyes were full of fire and fury. Determination and despair.

"If the judge says I have to go with Aunt Paige, I won't go! I'll run away!"

With that, Bryan whirled and raced out the wide-open stable doors into the sunlight. He turned on the road and was quickly out of sight.

Removing his hat, Jay ran his fingers through his hair. Fear twisted in his gut. Fear that Bryan would do something stupid. Fear that Jay wouldn't be able to stop or protect the boy. He had to find a way to convince Paige that Bryan would be better off staying in Bear Lake. Or he had to propose a plan she could accept.

And even if he did come up with a compromise, there was no guarantee Bryan would go along with the deal.

The knot in Jay's gut wasn't going to let go any-time soon.

Chapter Nine

Bryan had already left for school when Jay came into the kitchen for breakfast. Paige was at the table drinking coffee. Her sandy-blond hair was still mussed from sleep, her face scrubbed clean of makeup. She'd pulled on one of Krissy's old T-shirts. The combination made her look sleepy and warm and just right for cuddling.

"Morning." Putting his earlier thought aside, Jay grabbed a bowl from the cupboard, poured himself some cereal and took a banana from the fruit bowl on the counter.

"Good morning." Her flat voice and the worry lines across her forehead suggested troubled thoughts.

He poured milk on his cereal and sat down. "I assume you're planning to visit Henry at the hospital this morning."

"Yes, someone needs to be there to protect the

nurses from his wrath. I don't think he's a very good patient."

"Probably not." He spooned some cereal into his mouth. He had to be careful how he phrased his next comment. "Bryan reached out to me yesterday. He's really upset about Henry being so sick. He thinks he should stay here to take care of Henry."

"That's so sweet of him to worry over Grandpa." Her faint smile traveled like a moonbeam right into his chest and pricked his conscience.

"He's dead set about not moving to Seattle with you." He cleared the uncomfortable lump in his throat. "He said if the judge ruled he had to go with you, he'd run away."

Paige set her coffee mug down hard and gaped at him. Her cheeks flushed a pretty pink. Then she gave her head a quick shake.

"All children run away at one time or another. Krissy ran away when she was four. She got on her tricycle and pedaled down the road. Some neighbor found her about four blocks away sobbing. They brought her home no worse for wear."

"I think Bryan's threat is a little more serious."

Leaning forward to make her point, Paige said, "Krissy ran away again when she was about ten. She spent the night in a neighbor's tree house. By morning she was hungry and came home on her own. Running away is a rite of passage for some kids."

"Did you ever run away?" Jay countered.

"Well, no. Not until I got my job in Seattle. That hardly counts as running away."

Jay wondered if that was true. Given her family's treatment of Krissy, Jay could only imagine that he would have wanted to get away as soon as possible in her position.

Leaning back, he exhaled in frustration. "I've been trying to think of some sort of a compromise that might be okay with Bryan."

"Like what?" A skeptical note sharpened her voice.

"Maybe something like shared custody. Bryan could live with you during the school year and spend summers and holidays here."

Her eyes widened and she pushed back her chair. "There was nothing in Krissy's letter that suggested I should be Bryan's part-time guardian. I'm confident once we get the details worked out, Bryan will be fine living with me. Of course, we'll come and visit. I know how much Bryan loves Grandpa."

Standing, she held his gaze for a moment before carrying her mug to the sink and rinsing it. "I'd better get showered and dressed. I want to get to the hospital early enough that Grandpa hasn't badgered the nurses too badly."

"Right." So much for shooting down his compromise without a second thought. "I'll be out at my truck whenever you're ready to go."

"There's really no need for you to come along.

I'm sure you have other work to do with the horses or something."

He carried his bowl over to the sink. "I care about Henry, too. I want to be there if he needs me."

With a curious look in her soft brown eyes, she nodded. "If that's what you want."

Jay wanted a bunch of things, starting with Paige understanding Bryan belonged right here in Bear Lake and ending with kissing her in a way that would go on for a long time.

Neither option seemed likely, however. In the mood she was in, a kiss might make her mad. Maybe madder than when he'd sneakily forced her into trying to saddle Bright Star. He smiled as he recalled how beautiful she'd been that day, giving him a piece of her mind.

"What are you smiling about?"

"Uh, nothing. You go get dressed. I'll be waiting for you." Waiting for the right time to kiss her again.

Paige entered the hospital room and found Grandpa sitting up in bed. His hair needed combing and his whiskers grayed his cheeks. The tray table next to his bed held a half-eaten breakfast.

"Good morning, Grandpa." She bent over to kiss him on his unshaven cheek. "How do you feel this morning?"

"Dandy," he grumbled. "When can I get out of this zoo? Folks kept waking me up all night wanting to take my temperature and sticking me with I don't know what all."

Jay took up a position opposite Paige, placing his hands on the guardrail. "Sounds like you're in fine form, Henry. We came to rescue the nurses from your bad humor."

"I'm the one who needs rescuing."

"Be nice," Paige said.

"Harrumph."

Jay placed a small leather case on the bed table. "I brought your shaving gear. That'll perk you right up. Let me get a towel from the bathroom and we'll get you back to your handsome, pink-cheeked self." He stepped into the bathroom.

"My cheeks haven't been pink—"

"I think it's very nice of Jay to give you a shave. I wouldn't have thought to bring your razor along this morning."

"If you had, I wouldn't've let you touch me. You probably would've slit my throat."

She laughed. The hospital stay had certainly turned him into a grumpy old man. But maybe he was simply worried about what the doctors might find.

Jay returned, lowered the bed railing and sat down beside Grandpa. "Turn your head away and be still. I don't want to cut you."

Paige watched as Jay lathered Grandpa's cheek. Then with great care he pulled the razor down, making a trail of smooth skin. She'd observed Jay's gentle touch with his horses. The way he had calmed them with quiet words of reassurance. But this was special. More loving. As if Jay was Henry's son, not simply a hired hand.

She hadn't realized how close the two men were. Apparently in the five years Jay had worked for Grandpa, they had bonded. She envied the closeness they shared.

Taking a copy of the day's Kalispell newspaper from the tray table, she sat down in a chair. But she was unable to take her mind off the intensity of Jay's attention to the job at hand.

She wondered what it would feel like to have Jay so intensely attentive to her. At the image she conjured, she felt a decidedly feminine response.

Quickly, she snapped the paper open and began to read the headline story about the decrease in gasoline prices and how that would impact tourism in the county.

Out in the hallway, she heard the passing laundry cart. Over the loudspeaker system, a disembodied voice paged Respiratory Therapy. The nurses in the nearby station chatted among themselves.

"There you go, boss." Jay used a towel to wipe the remaining shaving cream from Grandpa's wrinkled face. "You're all smooth and not a single drop of blood."

"*Huh!* Through no fault of yours, I'm sure."

"Say *thank you,* Grandpa," Paige reminded him.

He mumbled something under his breath that made Jay laugh.

Paige chewed on her lower lip. Jay had wanted her to consider a compromise that would make Bryan happy. Maybe she could convince Grandpa to sell the outfitting business and move to Seattle to be with her and Bryan. They'd be a loving family and she could take care of her grandfather.

Maybe Grandpa could even sell the property to Jay.

She frowned at the thought, realizing her idea would separate the two men and their close relationship. Would that even be fair?

Just then Dr. Johansen stepped into the room. "How's our patient doing?"

Paige stood. "We've been giving the nurses a break from his grumpy disposition."

"I heard that," Grandpa groused.

The doctor shot Paige a boyish grin and nodded to Jay before turning his attention to Grandpa. "In that case, Mr. Stephenson, we'll take pity on our fine nursing staff and send you home."

Immediately alert, Grandpa sat up straight. "'Bout time. Bring me my pants, girl."

"Hang on a minute." The doctor handed Paige several sheets of paper with discharge instructions. "We've gotten all your tests back and your heart looks good."

"I could've told you that." Grandpa threw his bare, pale legs over the side of the bed.

"You still have a lot of fluid around your heart," the doctor continued as another doctor was paged over the loudspeaker. "That's what is making it hard for you to breathe. I've ordered three prescriptions for you to take at home."

"I don't need any pills," Grandpa objected.

"I'll make sure he takes his pills, Doctor," Paige promised, although she wasn't sure how long she'd be staying in Bear Lake. At least until after the guardianship hearing on Thursday. Then she'd have to find another solution.

"The fluid is putting a lot of pressure on your left ventricle." The doctor named the medication, which Paige checked on the prescription list he'd provided. "You'll also be taking a diuretic pill and another for your high blood pressure. Your granddaughter can pick them up at the pharmacy downstairs."

Grandpa responded with a grunt.

"And I want to see you in my office on Friday to gauge how you're doing."

"It'll be a waste of time. I'm feeling as fit as can be."

"I'd like to keep you that way, Mr. Stephenson." He extended his hand. Reluctantly, Grandpa took it, and they shook.

Turning to Paige, the doctor said, "If he gives

you a hard time, Miss Barclay, bring him back. My nurses know how to handle grumpy old men."

Grandpa mumbled something that sounded like an invective while Paige smiled and thanked the doctor. When he left, Paige said, "Do you want me to help you get dressed, Grandpa?"

"I've been dressing myself since I was as young as a newborn colt. You go get them fool pills and then get me out of here."

"Easy, Henry." Jay rested his hand on Grandpa's shoulder. "I'll help you get dressed while Paige goes for the prescriptions. We don't want you falling down and hitting that hard head of yours."

Grandpa acquiesced, but didn't look happy about it.

As Paige left the room, she decided she was glad Jay had come with her to the hospital. He had a way about him that kept Grandpa from flailing at the world out of frustration or maybe his fear of dying. An admirable talent.

By the time Paige returned from the pharmacy, Grandpa was dressed and sitting on the edge of the bed, Jay lounging beside him. A gray-haired volunteer in a blue jacket was there with a wheelchair. She looked vaguely familiar.

"Hello, Paige. I'm Adrienne Walker. We met at your sister's funeral. I'm the pastor's wife."

Her cheeks warmed. "Oh, yes, of course, Mrs. Walker. For a moment—"

"No need to apologize, dear. Funerals are so emotional, it's hard to remember who was there and who wasn't."

"I was very grateful for all your husband and the ladies of the church did for us."

"It's just part of our service in the Lord's name, dear."

Grandpa stood. "Could you two ladies stop your jabbering so I can go home?"

"That's what I'm here for, Henry." Adrienne adjusted the wheelchair so he could sit down. "Climb aboard."

"I don't need that thing. I can walk fine on my own."

"Sorry, but it's a hospital rule. No patient leaves without our escort service. Think of this as your personal chariot."

"Sit, Grandpa." Paige retrieved the vase of flowers she'd purchased at the gift shop downstairs. She reached for the bag of her grandfather's personal effects, but Jay got to it first. "The sooner you stop fussing, the sooner you'll be back home."

Once Paige got Grandpa home, she fed him some chicken soup for lunch. After he got most of the soup down, he pleaded fatigue and went to bed to take a nap. Jay had gone out to see to the horses, leaving Paige on her own.

With nothing specific on her to-do list, and Bryan not home, she got out a mop and pail from the mud-room and scrubbed the sticky kitchen floor.

While the floor dried, she went down the hall and stopped in front of Krissy's closed bedroom door.

Near the hospital she'd noticed Second Time Around, a thrift shop supporting Bear Lake Medical Clinic. That seemed like a good organization to support. Grandpa had suggested she take on the task of cleaning out Krissy's room if she had time. When she checked with Bryan, he'd given her an indifferent shrug.

Swallowing hard and bracing herself against the threat of tears, she opened the door and went to the closet. The jumble of shoes and boots remained on the floor; tops, pants and dresses hung every which way.

Paige flicked open a large trash bag. She dragged a flannel shirt off its hanger, folded it neatly and placed it in the bag. Somewhere in Krissy's room there would be items she'd keep for Bryan—scrapbooks and jewelry, but not these worn clothes.

The faint scent of horses and Krissy's lemony shampoo filled her nostrils as she worked her way methodically through the clothing. Jeans went in the bag. A nice pair of khaki slacks. An old sweater with two buttons missing.

She heard a truck door slam shut, and wondered if they had company.

Setting the bag of clothing aside, she left the bedroom. As she walked into the living room, Bryan appeared from the kitchen.

"Hi! How did you get home so soon?" She glanced out the window trying to spot the truck she'd heard.

"Jay picked me up at the bus stop. Is Grandpa home?"

"He is. He's napping right now. I imagine he'll be up soon."

"Is he…" Worry puckered his forehead. "Is he okay?"

"He has to take some medications, but the doctor thinks he'll be fine if he does as he's been told."

"I'll make sure he does," Bryan said in a determined, grown-up voice.

Smiling, she skimmed her hand over the boy's sweaty head. "Me, too."

He eased away from her. "Can I see him?"

"I don't want you to wake him if he's still asleep."

"I'll be quiet." He hurried down the hall.

Paige appreciated Bryan's obvious love and concern for his great-grandfather. Grandpa had always been like a father to the boy. A steady influence who gave his love unconditionally.

Her stomach knotted, imagining how Bryan would feel to leave Grandpa. But maybe that wouldn't happen. If her idea worked and she could convince Grandpa to sell the outfitting business and move to Seattle with her, they could all be together.

Then what would happen to Jay? She couldn't picture him living anywhere but right here with mountains and streams and wilderness in his backyard. Could he buy the outfitting business? Or find another job nearby?

She heard Grandpa and Bryan talking in the bedroom, Grandpa insisting he was as fit as he'd ever been, Bryan not quite buying his story.

She decided this was a good time to pose a compromise position that she could live with. Putting her boots on in the mudroom, she headed for the barn.

Jay picked up a bridle and started to polish it. He and Nathan were scheduled for an afternoon trail ride tomorrow. Just as well he made sure the tack was in order.

Footsteps on the gravel walkway preceded Paige's arrival. She stopped at the open barn door, her feminine figure silhouetted by the afternoon sun.

Jay swallowed hard. He squeezed the polishing rag harder. Just seeing her there gave him an urge to pull her into his arms and hold her.

Knowing that he had to stop Paige from taking Bryan away, *for Bryan's sake,* prevented him from giving into the impulse.

"There you are." Paige strolled toward him, her hips swaying gently with each step. "Bryan said you'd given him a ride home from the bus stop."

He cleared his throat. "I had to make a quick run into town for some electrical tape. I was just pulling into the road when I saw the school bus coming. Figured I'd save him a few steps."

"He went right in to see Grandpa. Poor kid is so worried about him." She snared a bridle from its peg and picked up a polishing rag. "Cleaning tack seems to be a full-time job around here."

"Pretty much. We've got a trail ride scheduled for tomorrow. Figured I'd better check the tack. Is Henry okay?"

"He was tired. I fed him soup and then he went to his room for a nap. The doctor seemed to think he'll be fine."

"For an eighty-five-year-old."

"That's true." Paige pursed her lips, understanding what Jay was trying to say. She had no way to refute the truth, only to ignore it. For the moment. "You didn't come in for lunch. If you're hungry, I can fix something for you."

"It's okay. I grabbed a burger at the Peewee Drive-In when I was in town." He hooked the bridle back in place. "I'm going to take Thunder Boy for a ride. He hasn't been out for two days and needs the exercise."

Focusing on the bridle she was cleaning, Paige

searched for the right words to broach her idea. "I've been thinking about your compromise suggestion."

His head snapped up. "You have?" He looked far more eager than she liked.

"I have a countersuggestion. Clearly Grandpa is getting on in years. He's going to be needing help soon. I thought I'd talk to him about selling the business and moving to Seattle with me and Bryan."

Jay's jaw dropped open. "Are you kidding me?

"Not a bit." His reaction surprised her. After all, coming up with a compromise was his idea. "Living with Grandpa would help Bryan to adjust to his new home in Seattle. They'd be together, and I could take care of them both."

"Think of this for a minute." His voice was patient but his brows were about as low as they could go, shadowing his eyes. "How well do you think Henry is going to adjust to living in a condo? He's lived here all of his life. He's got acres of land he can roam. His closest neighbor is a half mile away."

"That's exactly the point." She matched his reasonable tone with her own argument. "He needs to be around people who can check on him. Look after him."

Jay tossed his cleaning rag aside. "I can look out for Henry. And Bryan. Right here where they have lived all of their lives. You can talk to Henry if you want to. But I guarantee he won't agree to move to

Seattle. The best thing for everyone concerned is to let Bryan stay here where he belongs."

"I guess we'll see, won't we?"

Paige carefully put down her cleaning rag and hung up the bridle. Jay Red Elk didn't know the meaning of the word compromise. He wanted the world on his terms; no one else's mattered.

She wasn't going to *compromise* if it meant giving up her guardianship rights. She was doing what Krissy had wanted. She had to. Because it was the *right* thing to do.

And she'd always been the *good* sister.

After Paige left the barn, Jay worried some saddle soap into one of the older saddles.

He didn't know what he was going to do if Paige didn't give some ground on the guardian business. Moving Henry to Seattle sure wasn't the answer.

Jay knew he had to do something. Deep down he felt Bryan would make good on his threat to run away. Outside of tying the kid up and stuffing him in Paige's trunk, he didn't know how to stop the boy.

Obviously Paige thought otherwise.

Maybe he needed another approach if he was going to change her mind.

Paige served everyone their dinner and sat down at her place. After a silent grace, she picked up her fork.

"Grandpa, do you want some more mashed potatoes?" Bryan asked. Instead of his usual place at the dinner table, he'd moved closer to his great-grandfather.

"I'm good, son. Got more on my plate than I can handle already."

Paige cut a bite of oven-baked chicken breast, forked it into her mouth and chewed thoughtfully. No question, Bryan wasn't going to let Grandpa more than a few feet away from him until he was back to good health. He hadn't even checked on Bright Star since he'd come home from school. Sweet boy.

Yet that very sweetness and concern made it harder than ever for Bryan to agree to move to Seattle. At least, not without Grandpa.

"Maybe after dinner we can play a game," Bryan suggested to Grandpa.

"Not one of your video games." Shaking his head, Grandpa pushed his plate away. He had left half of what he'd been served. "My reflexes aren't as good as yours."

"How about checkers? Or we could all play Monopoly." He shot a pleading look toward both Paige and Jay, who had been unusually quiet throughout dinner.

"Are you up to it, Grandpa?" Paige asked.

"You know what I'd like, girl? I'd like to sit in my chair peaceful as can be and listen to you play the piano like your grandmother did." He gave a sharp nod. "That's what I'd like."

The eager spark in Bryan's eyes dimmed.

Paige wished Grandpa had accepted the boy's invitation to play a game. Bryan was trying so hard to take care of him.

"If it's music you want," she said, "we can start off with Bryan's and my 'Chopsticks' duet. How does that sound?"

"That'd be fine." Grandpa shoved his chair back and stood.

Bryan immediately jumped up beside him. "I'll help you to your chair, Grandpa. Put your arm around my shoulder."

Instead of doing as Bryan asked, Grandpa ruffled the boy's hair. "I'm not a cripple yet, youngster. I still got two good feet and the will to use 'em." He gave the boy a one-armed hug, and they walked together into the living room.

Pursing her lips together, Paige fought the impulse to tell Bryan he could stay with his grandpa forever and ever. But if she was to be his guardian, she needed to work. Her job was in Seattle. Therefore, she had to return to the city with Bryan. And maybe Grandpa, as well.

Picking up his plate and glass, Jay stood. "I'll take care of the dishes. You go ahead, play the piano with Bryan and entertain Henry."

"We can get the dishes done faster with two of us."

"I've got this. Go on and do your thing." He turned on the water to rinse his plate, then ran the garbage disposal.

The racket made it impossible for him to hear her. His silent dinner suggested he didn't want to talk to her at all. He wanted to avoid her.

Because he didn't like her idea of compromise.

A troubled sigh escaped her lungs.

In the living room, she enticed Bryan to join her at the piano. They ran through "Chopsticks" several times before he got bored. Then he plopped himself in the upholstered chair next to Grandpa in his recliner. Being physically close to Grandpa seemed to give Bryan comfort, so Paige didn't complain. As he saw Grandpa's health improving, surely his fears would ease.

In the bookcase near the piano, she found some sheet music of old familiar tunes: "Beautiful Dreamer" and "Oh, Susanna!" and "Home on the Range." Tunes Grandma Lisbeth had played.

At one point as she was playing, she glanced toward the kitchen doorway. Jay was standing there watching her, his expression unreadable. Their eyes met for a moment. When she smiled, he walked slowly toward her, his dark eyes never leaving hers.

The hair on her nape reacted as though lightning

was about to strike. Her fingers missed the keys. She stopped playing. In the silence, she heard her blood pulsing through her ears.

"How about you and me playing a duet?" he asked.

She swallowed and licked her lips. "You play the piano?"

"Sort of." He slid onto the piano bench beside her. His thigh pressed against hers. "Mom has a piano. All us kids tinkered at it. In junior high I took up the guitar, so I can read music."

"You play the guitar?"

"Not anymore. It was a rite of passage for twelve-year-olds back then. After that got old, we all took up rodeo riding in the junior division."

He shuffled through the stack of sheet music. "How 'bout this one." He put the music in place.

It was "Moon River." Slow and romantic.

"Looks good to me." Her fingers trembled slightly as she placed them on the keys.

"One, two, three." He nodded and they began, Jay playing the melody an octave higher than the written notes.

As they played along together, Paige became aware of the slow beat of her heart, matching the music, and the heat of Jay's thigh next to hers. She pictured a big Montana moon on the lake. The water glistening gold. Jay's arm around her.

Thoughts of guardianship and Bryan slipped from her mind, replaced by dreams of happily ever after. A dream she knew couldn't come true.

Chapter Ten

Breakfast was a quiet affair the following morning.

Paige lingered over her coffee. Jay had eaten early with Bryan, then Jay went out to take care of his business. Grandpa had drifted into the kitchen later. He'd had some cereal before assuming his position in front of the television for the morning news.

Paige knew she should check in with her boss. There was a midweek conference at the hotel for two hundred science and math teachers. Somehow she couldn't build up the energy to worry about the meeting. The teachers would surely behave themselves. Mr. Armstrong knew how to reach her if they didn't.

Picking up Grandpa's dirty cereal bowl, she went to the sink to rinse it and put it in the dishwasher along with her coffee mug. She turned on the water. All she got was a hiss of air.

"Well, that's strange." She'd had plenty of water when she brushed her teeth. What in the world…

She checked the bathroom off the mudroom. No water there, either. None in the master bathroom. She wandered back into the living room.

"Grandpa, I'm going to check something outside. Do you need anything?"

"Not unless you could straighten out those politicians back east." He tilted his head up to her. He was dressed in his jeans and a blue work shirt, but he hadn't shaved yet. "Something wrong?"

"I'm not sure. I'll be back in a minute."

She checked for water pressure in the hose that was hooked up at the back of the house. Barely a drop dripped out. She checked the faucet on the side of the barn.

Still no water.

Jay stepped out of the barn, his long legs encased in tight jeans, his hat tipped back on his head. "What's going on? You planning to water something?"

"Evidently you haven't noticed yet. We don't have any water pressure."

His brows scrolled downward. "Why not? We had pressure earlier."

"You're welcome to try." She gestured to the faucet she'd just worked. Strange he wouldn't take her word for it. That must be a guy thing.

He gave the faucet a twist. "No water in the house, either?"

"Not a drop."

"Guess we'll have to call Roy Taylor. He's the local plumber."

"Don't call him yet. Let me see if I can figure out what's wrong."

His grin turned incredulous. "Don't tell me you're a licensed plumber?"

With her hand, she flipped the tips of her hair. If only he knew she had all sorts of untapped talents. "My parents ran a hardware store. You'd be surprised how good I am with a screwdriver or a pair of pliers, and how many things I know how to fix."

"This I've gotta see."

"Watch and learn," she said with smug confidence. She glanced around. While working with her parents, she'd certainly learned a lot about wells that stopped pumping and how to fix them. The first thing was to check the power to the pump. "Do you know where the fuse box is?"

Archie trotted over to greet them, her tail wagging.

"Hi, little lady, how's your delicate condition today?" Paige asked, reaching down to pet the dog.

Archie sat and peered up at her, her brown eyes pleading for more attention.

"Fuse box is by the kitchen window," Jay said.

"Great." She strode off toward the house. She

might not be great with horses, but there had been more than one occasion at the hotel when she'd had to turn into a handyman.

Jay and Archie followed her. "I hope your plan doesn't include burning down the house. Or flooding the place."

"I'll try not to let that happen." She smiled at the sound of Jay's footsteps behind her and the relative peace and quiet of the forest as compared to the always present ambient noise in Seattle. When she searched for a new condo, she'd look for one that had a large patio. And she'd think about getting a small dog, both for herself and to keep Bryan company.

Or if Grandpa agreed to come along, she could buy a small house.

She lifted the cover on the fuse box. "Looks like someone planned ahead. They marked the fuse that relates to the well pump."

"Lots of smart people around here." Jay's teasing voice sent a tickle down her spine.

She threw the switch to cut off the power. "Now, do you know where the well is?"

"I think I can find it all right."

He headed off toward the back of the house.

"Here you are. One well house with a very quiet pump. Maybe if you turn the power back on, it'll start working again."

"Hmm. Maybe." She eyed the pressure gauge,

an old one which was stuck at zero. She gave it a flick with her finger. It didn't budge. Thus, the most likely source of the problem.

She looked up at Jay, who was standing so close she caught the scent of hay and horses. "I don't suppose you have a spare pressure gauge around, do you?"

He went back to scowling. "What makes you so sure the problem is the pressure gauge?"

"My father used to tell customers that replacing a pressure gauge was the simplest thing they could do and to do that first before they hauled the motor out of the well, which can be a major project."

"Okay." He pulled out his cell phone. "I'll call Roy. See when he can get over here. He's the local well guy, too."

"No, don't do that. If he's like most plumbers I've known, it'll take him a day or two before he gets around to coming over here, and we'll be without water until then." She closed the well house door. "It will be quicker and cheaper if I run into town and get one myself. They're not hard to replace."

"You're going to *replace* the pressure gauge *yourself?*"

She gave him a sweet smile. "Unless you'd like to do it and have the time."

His brows dropped down again. "I have to mail a package anyway. I'll take you into town."

"You don't have to. I can mail your package

for you while you stay here and keep an eye on Grandpa. I shouldn't be gone long."

"Nathan will watch Henry."

She wondered why he was so keen on driving her into town. Maybe he didn't think she knew what she was talking about when it came to well pumps. "If you insist. I'll get my purse and tell Grandpa where we're going."

She went into the house, feeling pretty smug. Men were always surprised when they realized she knew a lot about repairing stuff around the house. It did something to their macho image.

At least the thousands of hours she'd worked at the hardware store had given her that.

She checked on her grandfather. He seemed quite content watching TV.

"Grandpa, it looks like the well gauge is broken and we don't have any water. Do you think you'd be okay on your own if I ran into town with Jay to get a replacement gauge? We won't be gone long."

"We got a well man that does that kind of work."

"So I understand. But I think it'd be easier and quicker and cheaper if I can fix it myself."

Grandpa lowered his brows in a skeptical frown. "Go ahead, girl, if that's what you want. After this show is over, I thought I'd go sit out on the porch. Beginning to feel like I've been cooped up too long."

That was a good sign. Restlessness meant he was

feeling stronger. He seemed to be breathing more comfortably, too, so the medication was working.

"All right. But I want you to stay close to home. Nathan's out in the barn if you need anything. I don't want you wandering off by yourself. And don't try to fix the well on your own. It won't run at all until I replace the broken part."

He grunted in what she took to be an affirmative answer.

Jay climbed into his pickup, sat behind the wheel and placed the package to his mother on the dash. Who would have guessed a tiny little thing like Paige could replace a pressure gauge?

No matter what she said, he wasn't convinced she could. There was a lot of rust on the screws that held the gauge in place. It would take some arm strength to twist those screws out. It'd be easy to break one off. Then she'd have to drill the screw out, not an easy job and seriously frustrating. He knew that from experience.

He'd rather pay someone like Roy to do the job.

Paige climbed into the truck cab with a jaunty air and buckled her seat belt. "I'm ready to go."

He started the truck. "You sure you're not being a little overconfident? Replacing a pressure gauge can be harder than it looks. Particularly one that's been corroded over the years."

"We can get some Rust-Oleum while we're at the store. Unless you have some in your tool shop."

"I've got some around someplace," he grumbled. At least she knew what to do with rusty stuff. He'd have to give her that. But a woman like Paige, getting her hands dirty and wrestling with rusted screws? He was going to have to rethink his impression of her.

But knowing and doing were two different things. He was pretty sure he'd have to give her a hand. If nothing else, he'd have to make sure she didn't cross up the electrical wires when she put the new gauge in.

Jay angled into a parking spot in front of Carson's General Store and Paige climbed out, following him inside.

The narrow aisles made pushing a shopping cart a challenge. Periodic displays of canned goods or cereal boxes crowding into the aisles didn't help. But Paige had to admit the store carried a wide range of products, including a whole section devoted to fishing gear.

As she followed Jay toward the back, she noticed the postal annex in the far corner. Years ago, when Krissy had needed stamps, Paige had come with her to buy them. Not a particularly exciting outing.

She lingered back while he went up to the counter. "Hello there, young man." A short, stout woman who could barely see over the postal counter greeted Jay. "They must be keeping you busy with those horses."

"Most days, Valrie." He slid the package toward the clerk.

She checked the address. "Oh, how nice. Sending a present to your mother?"

"Her birthday's coming. I'd be in deep trouble if I didn't remember her."

"You surely would." Laughing, Valrie weighed the package. "Heavy for its size. What's she getting?"

"I spent a few evenings carving an eagle out of a chunk of wood."

"Oh, Jay," she cooed. "Aren't you the sweetest boy."

"If you say so, ma'am."

Paige noticed him turn his head away, embarrassed by the woman's fawning attention. For her part, Paige was impressed that he had the talent for carving. And he was thoughtful enough to give his mother a handmade gift. He got double points for that.

They finished their transaction and Jay stepped away from the counter.

Valrie spotted Paige. "Hello, dearie. Need any stamps today?"

"Not really. Thanks." Paige realized she was

the same woman who had been the postmistress years ago.

"Oh, you're Krissy's sister, aren't you? Such a shame what happened to her." The woman tut-tutted and fussed with her graying, upswept hairdo. "I recall simply shivering with fear when she'd drive down the street in her pickup. A million miles an hour and with all those people around. Poor dear, I thought she'd probably die in a car crash. You know, hit a deer and go off the road. But I'd never imagined her falling off a horse. Terrible."

Shuddering at the reminder of how Krissy had died, Paige glanced around for a means of escape.

"We had a car accident like that not too long ago," the postmistress continued. "Woman hit a tree when a deer jumped in front of her. Wrecked the car, but the woman and her daughter weren't hurt. That was a blessing."

"Valrie." Paige spoke her name in the hope she'd stop talking. "Can you tell me where I'd find the hardware section?"

"Of course. It's straight across." Valrie pointed to the opposite side of the store. "You can't miss it, dearie."

"Thank you so much." With a wave, Paige scurried away, ducking behind the bread display and out of Valrie's sight.

"What's the matter?" Jay joined her. "You didn't want to visit with Valrie for a while? You'd know everything about every resident of Bear Lake if you gave her a chance."

"I'm sure that's true. That woman could talk the glue off stamps if she had a mind to."

Jay laughed, a wonderfully infectious sound, and took her arm. The gesture sent a pleasurable ache wrapping around her heart.

They searched for a pressure gauge in the hardware section but found nothing that came close.

"Looks like we'll have to go over to Roy Taylor's after all. See if he's got what you need."

Pine Lane was only a few blocks from Main Street, the shop easy to find, Paige thought with amusement. A big yellow backhoe sat right in the front yard with a sign perched in its seat: Wells Dug Cheap.

Another sign hung on the open door to the shop: Gone Fishing. Take What You Need and Leave Me a Note.

Chuckling, Paige strolled into what turned out to be an oversize garage lined with shelves stuffed with various plumbing parts and supplies.

"Is Mr. Taylor always this trusting?" she asked.

Jay picked up a copper elbow pipe, weighed it in his hand, then returned it to the shelf. "I think it's more his devotion to fishing than his trust in humankind that makes him run his business this way."

"Apparently he doesn't get ripped off or he would have gone out of business a long time ago."

"The joy of living in a small town."

Aware of Jay watching her, Paige checked through various pressure gauges for the type she needed.

"Here it is." She held up the gauge to show him.

He peered at the device. "You sure it's the right kind?"

"Same brand as the old one. Nice big face to read the dial and the right size male connector."

The corner of his lips hitched up. "Maybe you do know what you're doing."

"Trust me, cowboy. When it comes to hardware, I'm an old hand."

Both chuckling, Jay wrote a note to Roy about their "purchase" and they left Roy's shop.

"You know something?" Jay slung his free arm around Paige's shoulder as they walked back to the truck. "Shopping with you is a lot more fun than shopping with a guy."

Her smiled broadened, and she was inordinately pleased with his comment.

Once in the truck, Jay asked, "You need anything else for this project?"

"Not if you've got a good assortment of tools. We should be good. Besides, I don't want to leave Grandpa alone too long." Although, deep down, she was sorry to end their excursion. She liked shopping with Jay, too. Very much so.

* * *

Paige needn't have worried about Grandpa.

They found him sitting on the front porch in a wicker rocking chair. Sprawled on the floor beside Grandpa, Archie was keeping him company. The dog opened one eye to gaze at Paige.

"You get what you needed?" Grandpa asked.

"We did. Jay took me to Roy Taylor's shop. Did you know he leaves it open? People could come in and take anything they want."

"Yep. That's how the old coot likes to do business." He eyed Jay and the gauge he was holding. "You gonna help the little lady install that thing?"

"I get the sense she knows what she's doing. I'll just hang around in case she needs some manly assistance."

"In your dreams, fella." She headed for the toolshed, her head held high with the knowledge that Jay had recognized she had some skill as a handywoman.

Removing the old gauge wasn't as easy as she'd hoped. But with the help of a lot of Rust-Oleum, she managed.

After she installed the new gauge, she asked Jay to switch the fuse back on. She held her breath while she waited.

With a hum, the pump started to work.

"We've got water!" she shouted.

Jay came trotting back. He checked the pump. "Well, isn't that something! Congratulations."

He picked her up and twirled her around.

She screamed and laughed. "Put me down!" But she didn't really mean it. She liked the feel of his strong hands around her waist. The press of his chest against her. The breadth of the shoulders she clung to.

Carefully, he lowered her to her feet. "Nice work, Miss Barclay."

She was about to thank him in return, but before she could speak, his lips covered hers. His lips were gentle yet determined. It made her heart soar to be in his arms. To be kissed so thoroughly by such a strong, thoughtful man.

Yet she knew that being with Jay, being held in his arms for more than just this moment, was a fantasy that could never come true.

At dinnertime, Jay relished telling Bryan about Paige's accomplishment installing the new gauge. He was as proud of her as if she'd won a couple of blue ribbons in a rodeo.

"It wasn't that big a deal," she insisted between bites of steak. "It's not like I climbed Mount Rainier all by myself."

"I didn't think girls could fix stuff like that, Aunt Paige," Bryan said with a hint of awe in his voice.

He checked with Jay. "Do you know how to change a gauge thing?"

"Sure. I had to supervise her, of course. Didn't want her to make a mistake." He winked at her.

Paige sniffed with ladylike disdain. "Girls can do lots of things, Bryan. At the hotel where I work, you'd be surprised what I've had to fix, everything from microphones and loudspeakers to toilets that were overflowing. That isn't my favorite chore."

"I imagine not." Jay frowned. What kind of classy job did she have anyway? "I thought you coordinated conferences, not that you were the maintenance guy."

"Unfortunately, maintenance guys aren't on duty 24/7." She shrugged easily and reached for the butter for her potato. "When a conference is going on, I'm pretty much there all the time."

"Wow. You've gotta be smart to do all that stuff," Bryan said.

Her laughter floated around the room like a fresh mountain breeze. "I'm probably more stubborn than smart, honey. You gotta do what you gotta do."

Something tightened in Jay's chest. Before now, he wouldn't have guessed she was a woman unafraid of getting her hands dirty. All he had known about her was that she was afraid of horses and had a high-powered job in Seattle. He hadn't given her credit for having plenty of guts and determination. If it weren't for Bryan's wish to stay here in the mountains with Henry, and his threat to run away, Jay knew her strengths would make Paige a great guardian for the boy.

A great mother for any child.

That thought pulled him up short.

In his eagerness to deter her from being Bryan's guardian, he hadn't thought of her as a mother.

As tough and strong as his own mother. A woman he admired above all others. Except his Annie. She'd been brave, too. Even as he had driven her to the hospital. Even in so much pain, Annie had tried to reassure him everything would be all right. She and the baby would be fine.

She'd been so terribly wrong.

He wiped his mouth with his napkin to mask the emotion that welled up in him. A need that was sharp and painful. An ache that made it hard to swallow. A yearning that he'd long since suppressed to the furthest reaches of his awareness.

It dawned on Jay that he didn't want Paige to leave, to go back to Seattle. She was the kind of woman a man needs around, someone to lean on. Capable. And loving. He'd seen that in how she treated her grandfather and now how she looked after Bryan. For a moment, he was envious of the kid.

The fact that sooner rather than later she would leave struck him like a winter blizzard. He was chilled to the bone with the sense of emptiness.

He had no idea how to get her to stay.

* * *

The following morning, Paige went back to the bittersweet chore of cleaning out Krissy's room. She intentionally kept her feelings in check. Compartmentalizing her mind separate from her heart and the ache of emotion that filled her chest. She'd found a scrapbook with pictures of Bryan and his mom together as well as school report cards and pictures he'd colored as a young child. She set those aside to keep for Bryan.

As she was working, her cell phone chimed. She stuffed the contents of one of Krissy's dresser drawers into the third plastic bag she'd filled for the thrift shop and grabbed her cell. The number registered as her boss. She stifled a groan. *What now?*

"Yes, Mr. Armstrong?"

"Good morning, Paige. How are things going with you?" His voice was smooth and cosmopolitan with just a trace of a British accent.

She knew he was asking when was she coming back to the hotel. The grief she experienced with every bit of Krissy's life she threw out wouldn't concern Mr. Armstrong.

"The court hearing about the guardianship is still scheduled for tomorrow."

"After that you'll come home, right?"

"I imagine so. We'll have to gather up whatever Bryan wants to take with him to Seattle." Friday was the last day of school. She'd need to get his school records. Current medical records, too. "The move may be difficult for him. It's a little more complicated than simply stuffing a few things in a suitcase and away we go." That was a huge understatement. Paige prayed she could pull it off without too much trauma or drama.

"The thing is, Paige..." He hesitated. "Betsy's been filling in for you."

Paige waited for him to continue.

"She slipped in the hotel kitchen yesterday and had to go to the emergency room. She broke her ankle."

"Oh, I'm so sorry. Betsy's such a nice young woman." If some days less efficient than Paige would like.

"Yes, well, she's been doing a fine job filling in, too. But the truth is, I need you back this weekend. The National Association of Innkeepers is coming in on Friday. We've got to be on our toes, make a good impression. It's important for the image of Elite Hotel properties."

"Yes, I know." She'd booked the innkeepers' event and knew they were particularly fussy. One dust bunny under somebody's bed, and the news would hit Twitter like a tsunami. Elite Hotel's name would be mud in the world of innkeepers.

"Does that mean you'll be able to get here by Friday?"

"I'm not sure." How could she possibly pack up

Bryan and leave early Friday morning? "Friday is the last day of school for him. Bryan's only twelve, Mr. Armstrong. This will be a big change for him." And when she thought about it, going back to Seattle wasn't quite as enticing as it had once seemed. She'd miss the clear mountain air. The scent of pine trees.

And Jay, she admitted, her throat tightening at the thought.

"If this conference doesn't go well, it could cost us both our jobs."

The implied threat shook Paige. Taking time off for a personal crisis shouldn't cost her a job she loved, a career she'd spent years training for. She had hoped the hotel management would be flexible.

"So can I count on you being here by noon on Friday?" Armstrong asked, although it sounded like an order.

"I'll try my best, sir."

"Fine." He disconnected the call without saying good-bye.

Staring at the silent phone, Paige sat down heavily on Krissy's bed. Maybe she could run to Seattle for the weekend and be back at Bear Lake by Monday. That would give Bryan an extra day or so to adjust to the reality of moving to Seattle. With a little luck she might find time to rearrange her home office into a bedroom that would do until she could find a bigger place for them.

Yes, that could work.

Leaning her head back, she tried to rub the tension from her neck. Two weeks ago the boss needing her would have been a thrill. One more step forward on her career path. She would have changed any appointment, any obligation, to race back to the hotel. To make any conference a grand success.

Now she wished the innkeepers would cancel their annual affair.

With a sigh, she decided she needed some fresh air.

Grandpa had been feeling much better this morning and had gone out to the barn to putter. Nathan and Jay were both working nearby, so they'd been keeping an eye on Grandpa.

Still, she hated the thought of leaving Grandpa when he wasn't one-hundred-percent well.

The warmth of the sun hinted at an early summer. So did the purple lupines and wild alpine daisies that had sprung up almost overnight in a nearby open field. She inhaled deeply and caught the suggestion of flowers perfuming the air.

Around the hotel, the flowers were all hybrids engineered to be easy to care for, and the only natural scent that came along was when the lawns were freshly mowed. She'd always enjoyed that smell.

Now, to her dismay, she preferred the scent of wild flowers and pine trees.

The smell of horses and manure not so much, she thought as she walked into the barn.

"Hey, Paige." Jay, standing in Thunder Boy's stall, touched the brim of his hat. "You come out to take a ride on Peaches? It's been a couple days."

She glanced around, spotting Nathan cleaning a nearby stall and Grandpa sitting by the tack room polishing a saddle.

"Not really." She didn't want either Nathan or Grandpa to see how awkward she was on a horse.

"Go ahead, girl. Sweet Peaches won't hurt you," Grandpa said.

Jay ducked out of Thunder Boy's stall. "I'll get her saddled and ready for you."

"No!" Her sharp retort stopped Jay in his tracks and embarrassed Paige. She wasn't afraid of Peaches. Not like she had been before. She didn't want Jay and Grandpa to think she was. She'd been the target of their amusement one too many times. At least Bryan wasn't here if she made a fool of herself. Again.

Raising herself to her full five feet five, plus the height of her boot heels, she said, "I'll saddle Peaches myself, thank you."

She marched into Peaches's stall and led the horse into the corral, looping the lead rope over the railing. Archie immediately showed up as if she knew something special was about to happen.

"I know what I'm doing," she said under he

breath as much to herself as to the dog. "I'm not going to fall off this time."

Archie's only answer was to increase the beat of her wagging tail.

She hauled the saddle, bridle and blanket from the tack room, acknowledging Grandpa's wink and smile with a quick nod. Sweet Peaches accepted the bit without any fuss.

When Paige hefted the saddle onto the horse, Peaches danced sideways a couple of steps. Paige stopped her with a curt *whoa* and settled the saddle into place.

All the while she was aware of eyes following her every movement. Nathan. Grandpa. And most assuredly Jay.

Paige would only be here a few more days. She vowed she wasn't going to leave them with an impression of her incompetence on a horse. Or any other way.

Mounting easily, she reined Peaches around to circle the corral. That would show them. She was no scaredy-cat.

Out of nowhere, Jay showed up right next to her on Thunder Boy.

She started, jerking the reins sideways. "What are you doing?"

Jay's grin flashed white teeth. "Going for a ride with you."

"I don't need an escort, thanks. I'm taking a turn around the corral. That's all."

"I thought I'd take you to a place I know. You'll like it." They'd reached the gate. Jay leaned over, unlatched it and pushed the gate open.

Paige hesitated. He wanted her to ride out of the corral? On Peaches? A thousand scenarios, all of them potentially disastrous, flicked through her imagination like an old movie when the film started flapping off-kilter. How could she—

"You coming or not?" He tipped his hat back. His eyes zinged her with a challenge.

She licked her lips. "All right. But we shouldn't go far. Grandpa—"

"He's fine. Nathan will keep an eye on him." Taking his hat off, Jay waved her through the open gate as though ushering her into a fine restaurant.

Her stomach tightened but not from hunger. Relaxing her death grip on the reins, she gave Peaches a nudge with her heels.

Trotting, Archie went with her out of the corral.

Chapter Eleven

"Relax your seat. Enjoy the ride." Riding beside Paige, Jay had taken the trail past the main house. He figured with the court hearing tomorrow this could well be the only chance he'd have to show her his special place, the natural cathedral he'd found.

After tomorrow, she could well be on her way back to Seattle with Bryan. Or she could hate Jay for blocking her plan, if it came to that.

"If I relax my seat, my spine is going to turn into overcooked spaghetti."

Jay stifled a laugh. "That might be a little too relaxed. Just kind of lean back in the saddle. Let your body move with the rocking motion. Keep your reins loose." While Paige would never be a natural rider, he was amazed how much progress she'd made since her first up-close encounter with Bryan's horse, Bright Star.

He watched as her hair bounced against her cheek

with each stride the horse took. His fingers itched to slip through the silky strands.

"What if Peaches decides to take off at a run? That will unrelax me in a hurry."

"She won't do anything you don't tell her to. Unless she gets spooked by a bear or something."

Paige's head snapped around. She glared at him. "That's the second time you've said something about bears. You're just trying to spook me, aren't you? There aren't really any bears, are there?"

"Don't worry. Yeah, there are bears around here. But if they're nearby, they'll hear us coming and take off before we even see them." Usually that was the case. But springtime and hungry bears could be an unpredictable combination. The bear he'd spotted yesterday was on the far side of the hill. Probably still sleeping off the big meal he'd eaten. Chances were good there weren't any other bears in the area. Except that it was close to mating season. A male bear could travel a long distance to sniff out a mate.

Archie raced off after a squirrel. With a warning wiggle of its tail, the squirrel scampered up a tree. He perched on a branch out of Archie's reach and chattered at the dog.

"Does Archie ever actually catch a squirrel?" Paige asked.

"She used to. Now she just chases them for sport. Keeping in shape, I imagine."

"Huh. She ought to leave the poor little things alone. They're cute."

The squirrel chase appeared to have relaxed Paige a little. She was sitting more comfortably in the saddle. The reins looser even though she still had one hand on the saddle horn. She held her head high, her chin at a determined angle that made Jay smile. He hated the thought that, one way or another, she'd be leaving Bear Lake soon.

"Where are we going?" she asked.

"There's a lookout up ahead with a clear view of the lake. Then, if you're up to it, we can go on to the natural cathedral I mentioned."

Her brown eyes widened, sparkling like she'd just awakened to Christmas morning. "Really? How far is it?"

"It'll take us about forty-five minutes to get there."

Her forehead furrowed. "Okay. I guess that means my muscles will need a long, hot soak in the tub by the time we get back home."

His lips twitched at the enticing image that conjured. He quickly refocused his attention on the turnoff to the overlook a few feet up the trail.

Paige fell in behind Jay as he turned onto a narrower trail. Pine branches brushed against her arm. A small brown bird flew past her right at eye level. She smiled as the tiny creature darted and twisted its way through the maze of overlapping tree branches.

In a matter of minutes, they broke out of the forest into a cleared area. Bear Lake appeared in front of them, a brilliant reflection of the blue sky. Paige drew in a deep breath.

"It's beautiful." Pristine. Primitive in the way nature had carved the rugged hillsides into an irregularly shaped bowl to gently contain the glistening water.

"Yeah, it is." Jay hooked one leg over his saddle horn and pointed toward the west. "Town is over that way. You can see the highway that runs through town and the layout of the residential areas."

The highway wound its way from the south, vanishing from view behind a hill north of town. From this distance, the homes looked like dollhouses set on tiny ribbons that were streets.

"Across the lake from town, there's Arrowhead Cove." Jay pointed to a bay on the east side of the lake. "Folks like to go there for picnics. There are a lot of summer cabins along that side of the lake, most of them hidden by trees. Everyone has a dock. Sometimes on holiday weekends there's a real traffic jam with speedboats and sailboats, water-skiers and kayaks swarming all over the place."

Today, Paige noted, the lake looked placid and welcoming. Only three boats were cutting wakes through the clear water.

"You can't quite make it out," he continued, "but at the far end of the lake is the town of Polson. It's not as pretty as Bear Lake but there's some good fishing down that way."

"I can see why you like to live here." But could she ever make the area her permanent home? That seemed impossible. For one thing, what would she do for a living? Turning herself into a back-country trail guide wasn't a plausible choice.

After a few minutes, Jay led her to the main trail and they continued up the hill. On an open slope covered with low vines, tiny blue flowers peeked out, looking fragile against a gray background of granite debris. Lodgepole pines shaded spruce and fir trees as the forest thickened again.

Jay pointed to the top of one of the pine trees. There, perched majestically on the highest branch, his white head clearly visible, a bald eagle gazed off into the distance.

Paige wondered if there was a nest nearby with baby hatchlings to feed.

As she rode, her gaze kept returning to Jay riding ahead of her. His broad back. The way his muscles flexed. The tilt of his cowboy hat. Definitely a man's man.

The trail wound downward, and soon they were enveloped by trees that blocked out the sun. She had no idea whether they were heading north or east or south. In the distance, she heard a roaring noise like cars racing around a track.

"What's that sound?" she asked.

He glanced over his shoulder. "You'll see in a minute."

The noise became progressively louder until they broke out of the trees high on a cliff. Below them a boiling river of water raced through a narrow canyon confined by steep vertical walls. Above them, thousands of gallons of water leaped off a cliff higher than the one where they were, plummeting into the canyon below.

Jay's cathedral. It was all she had imagined and more.

He dismounted, looped his horse's reins over a nearby branch, and came back to help her down from Peaches. Her legs wobbled. She grimaced.

"We'll stretch our legs for a minute." Cupping her elbow, he edged her forward to get a better view.

"This really is incredible." In awe, she gazed at the scene of power and glory, nature's wonder, and understood why Jay would feel close to God here. She felt His magnificent spirit here, too.

Archie trotted up to explore for new scents, sniffing at the ground and around the trees.

Jay looped his arm around Paige's shoulders. "This is the headwaters of Moccasin Creek, which flows into Bear Lake. It's still carrying a lot of snowmelt from the higher mountains. In the fall the waterfall isn't quite as spectacular as it is in the late spring."

"Then I'm glad you brought me here now." Her voice was husky with wonder, her senses overflowing, her heart filled with the rightness of being here with Jay. Sharing this moment together. This place of God's grace.

He turned her slightly, lifted her chin and she looked up into his intense blue-green eyes now dark with need.

"Whenever I've come here, it was to pray and remember Annie. Losing her and our son almost killed me. There were times when I didn't think I could go on. That's why I sold my ranch and took Henry's job. There were too many memories around my ranch."

He ran the back of his fingers down her cheek. "Lately, I've been thinking a lot about you."

Slowly, almost as though he were afraid she'd turn away, he lowered his head to hers. With the first brush of his lips, she shuddered in anticipation. He drew her closer. She lifted her arms around his neck. Her fingers threaded through the thick hair at his nape. She'd never felt quite like this before. Had never before wanted a kiss to go on forever.

Had never before fallen in love.

That realization stunned her. How could she possibly—

There was no way they could—

Did he mean that he was ready for a new relationship? That he'd let go of his memories of his wife?

She had no answers to her questions. But it didn't matter. Their lives were so different. City and country. Seattle and Bear Lake. The distance was insurmountable. Wasn't it?

It took all of her will to step away. His eyes even darker than before, he brushed a wayward strand of hair from her cheek. Goose bumps sped down her arms.

"You okay?" His whispered words shimmered through her like sparkling drops of clear water tumbling over a cliff.

"I'm fine." She cleared her throat. "Should we head back now?"

Slowly, he nodded. "I guess we'd better."

He helped her mount Peaches. She groaned as she straddled the horse again and he shot her a rakish grin.

"Remember the hot tub soak at the end of trail."

"I can hardly wait!" But she couldn't bear the thought of washing away the imprint of Jay's lips on hers. His taste. Or the sensation of being in his arms.

Loping ahead of them, Archie seemed to know they were heading home. Paige envied the dog's sure sense of where she belonged.

Henry and Bryan cooked hamburgers on the grill for dinner. They were blackened and hard as hockey pucks, but Jay was glad Henry had felt up to the task. He was breathing better these days and able to walk farther without having to pause.

Good for Dr. Johansen.

Slathering the burger with ketchup, Jay managed to finish off one hamburger. But his appetite wasn't up to par. His guilty secret made it hard for him to swallow. Tomorrow could well change everything.

He watched as she tasted one of the frozen French fries Bryan had heated in the oven. She wrinkled her nose, a funny little habit he'd noticed when she didn't approve of something.

"This afternoon I made a few calls," Paige said. "I found a Mrs. Murphy who does some house-keeping for local families. She's going to come by in the morning—"

"What do we need that old woman for?" Henry asked.

"I'm going to have her thoroughly clean and scrub Krissy's room. She'll make your lunch for you, too, while we're in Kalispell for the court hearing."

"I can make my own lunch," Henry grumbled.

"Am I going to Kalispell, too?" A deep frown worried Bryan's forehead.

"I think you should," Paige said. "The judge may want to ask you some questions."

"I'm going, too," Jay said.

Paige's brows rose. He hadn't told her he was coming along. Or why he would need to.

The boy's lower lip jutted out. "I'm going to tell him I'm not going to Seattle no matter what."

"I'd better go with you, too," Henry said. "No need for me to stay here and have an old woman fuss over me."

"She's not going to fuss over you, Grandpa. Besides it's a long trip up and back. It would wear you out." She turned to Bryan. "I know you're still upset about the move, but I promise we'll work it out. Seattle isn't the end of the world, you know."

Her voice had a soft, soothing quality, but Bryan wasn't buying it. He grabbed his plate and carried it to the kitchen counter. The plate clattered on the tile.

"The judge will listen to me. I'll make him listen." He whirled and marched out the back door.

Paige's face paled. "I wish there was something I could do to help him understand."

Jay shoved his plate aside. "It's not too late to consider an alternative. Shared custody. Something that would help Bryan."

Slowly, she glanced at Grandpa then shook her head. Jay was right. Grandpa would never agree to moving to Seattle.

"We've had this discussion before," she said to Jay. "Krissy wanted me to raise Bryan. It's the one thing I can do for her, and I intend to do it to the best of my ability. Besides, I love my nephew, pouty lower lip and all."

Jay couldn't hold her gaze. He got up and started

the kitchen cleanup. She'd earned the right to be Bryan's guardian. She'd done everything she could to get to know the boy. She'd stayed here for nearly two weeks when she probably should have gone back to Seattle to protect her job.

Maybe she was right. Bryan would have more opportunities in Seattle. Better schooling. A chance to see the Mariners play in person. Hear a symphony. Go to first-run movies without driving as far as Kalispell.

Bryan would have a good life with Paige.

But would Bryan make good on his threat to run away? If the boy headed to the high country, he might try to stay out there on his own.

A knot twisted in Jay's gut. How could he stop Bryan if the boy was determined to go off on his own? The kid was only twelve! He couldn't survive for long by himself.

When the kitchen was back in order, Jay went out to his quarters. He dropped down on the lumpy couch and stared at the photograph of his beloved wife.

"What should I do, Annie? Paige is a good woman. I think you'd like her. She's a strong woman like you were."

Leaning back, he scrubbed his hands over his face. How could he objectively weigh what Bryan wanted versus Paige's desire to follow her sister's wishes? There seemed to be no good answer. No middle ground.

Night began to creep in through the windows. He was about to turn on a light when there was a knock on the door.

Jay's heart skipped a beat. *Paige?*

He switched the light on and hurried to open the door.

Not Paige. *Bryan.*

"What's wrong?" Jay asked.

"I wanted to tell you I'm running away tonight. After everybody's asleep." Bryan looked him right in the eye.

A full-blown panic attack spurred Jay to action. He yanked the boy inside and closed the door behind him. "You can't do that. Where would you go? How are you going to take care of yourself? What are you going to eat? Where are you going to sleep?"

"I'll be okay." The boy stared at the floor, his voice not as cocky as it had been a minute ago.

It dawned on Jay that Bryan had come here hoping Jay would talk him out of his plan. He relaxed a little.

"Look, kid." Jay put his hands on Bryan's shoulders and looked into the boy's troubled eyes. "It's going to be okay tomorrow. It's just a hearing. It's not like Paige is going to stuff you in her car and drag you off to Seattle right after the meeting." Jay would do his best to stop that if the worst happened.

"But what if she does? It'll be too late for me to run away then."

Jay didn't want to give Bryan too much hope. But he had to find a way to stop him from acting tonight. Then maybe there would be time to work things out.

"Look, how about I talk to the judge? Maybe he can come up with an idea to keep you here."

"You'd do that?"

"I'll do my best. But no promises. Okay?"

Bryan threw his arms around Jay. "Thank you, thank you," he sobbed. "I wanna stay here with you and Grandpa. You won't let some judge send me away, will you?"

Jay cupped the boy's head where it rested against his shoulder. In so many ways, Bryan was the son he'd never had. He'd been watching the boy grow into a strong, smart, fine young man for the past five years. Jay didn't want to lose him anymore than Bryan wanted to go. He loved him.

So did Paige.

But what of his feelings for Paige? Chances were they would fall on deaf ears.

The clock tower of the old Flathead County Courthouse in Kalispell stood out above the turn-of-the-century three-story building. The actual courts, however, had been moved across the street to the Justice Center.

Jay found a spot in the parking lot, and the three of them went inside.

Waiting in the hallway for the case to be called, Paige noticed Bryan fidgeting. He couldn't seem to keep his feet still. He rotated his head on his shoulders. Picked at a scab on his elbow. Glanced constantly at Jay as though looking for reassurance.

He'd been that way during the entire ride to Kalispell.

Both Jay and Bryan had dressed in good jeans. Jay wore a blue dress shirt with the cuffs rolled up, Bryan a red T-shirt with "Grizzlies" stenciled on the front. Paige was wearing the one outfit she'd brought to Bear Lake suitable for business. Or a funeral.

Several people were waiting along with them, including family groups. Most looked eager and hopeful.

In contrast, Paige's stomach was on a rampage. Her chest felt tight. She'd fiddled with the latch on her purse so much it was a wonder she hadn't broken it.

This could well be the most important day of her life. And Bryan's.

Finally a court clerk called them in. The room was small, nothing like a courtroom used for a jury trial. The gray-haired judge, dressed in a business suit, sat at a conference table, a stack of file folders next to him. A nameplate announced he was the Hon. T. S. Willinger.

Chairs were arranged at the table opposite him. Paige gestured for Bryan to sit next to her but he demurred, claiming a chair beside Jay, leaving Paige feeling like it was two against one.

The court clerk sat to the judge's right ready to record the hearing on her steno machine.

"Good morning," Judge Willinger said with a friendly smile. He nodded toward Paige. "I take it you are Paige Barclay, who has requested that you be named guardian of…" He acknowledged Bryan with another nod. "Bryan Barclay, your nephew."

"Yes, sir."

He turned his attention to Jay. "And you are…?"

"Jay Red Elk. I'm, um…" He glanced at Bryan. "A friend. I work for Bryan's great-grandfather."

The judge sifted through the forms Paige had submitted. "This all looks pretty straightforward. Based on the written request of the deceased mother of Bryan Barclay, his aunt, Miss Paige Barclay, has asked to be named Bryan's guardian." He gave Bryan a pleasant smile. "You're a lucky young man to have your aunt—"

"I don't want her to be my guardian!" Bryan blurted out.

Judge Willinger's brows rose by an inch, and his forehead creased. "I beg your pardon?"

Tears filmed Bryan's brown eyes. "She's gonna

take me to Seattle and make me stay there with her. I don't want to go. I want to stay here with Jay and my great-grandpa." His voice sounded incredibly young. "He needs me."

I need you too, Paige almost burst out.

"Great-grandfather? You've mentioned him twice." The judge questioned both Jay and Paige.

"Your Honor, my grandfather, Henry Stephenson," Paige responded forcefully, "is eighty-five years old and in fragile health. He himself suggested to my sister that I be named Bryan's guardian should anything happen to her. That in itself should be reason enough to appoint me as guardian. As I noted in my application, I have included a copy of Kristine's will in her own handwriting to back up that statement."

"Interesting." The judge turned back to Bryan. "How old are you, young man?"

"I'm twelve." The boy turned to Jay, his eyes frantic, tears now oozing down his cheeks. "You promised you'd stop her. Not let her take me away."

Paige glared at Jay. *He'd promised?*

"Your Honor," Jay began as he reached his arm around Bryan's shoulders. "Bryan wants to stay in Bear Lake where he was born and has lived all of his life. I think that would be best for him. Because of that, I'd like to apply to be Bryan's guardian."

"What?" Her face heating with shock, Paige

shifted in her chair and gaped at Jay. "You can't do that. Krissy wanted me—"

"I tried to talk you into a compromise. Shared guardianship or something. But you wouldn't hear of it. I'm sorry, Paige." His gaze darted to the judge.

"You're sorry?" she gasped. The pain of Jay's action was like a slap to her face. It took her breath away. "What about Krissy's wishes? Bryan's mother wanted *me* to raise him. You're not even a blood relative."

Judge Willinger cleared his throat. "Let's remain calm, shall we?"

Paige turned on the judge. "I'm trying to fulfill my sister's last wish and you want me to remain calm?" Just yesterday Jay had kissed her. For the second time! He'd made her fall in love with him. And all the time he'd been plotting to become her nephew's guardian. Plotting to break her heart. How could he?

"Please, Miss Barclay." His eyes sympathetic, the judge held up a hand to quiet her.

Seething, she sat back in her chair. Of course Jay hadn't been pleased about her moving Bryan to Seattle. She understood that. But to go so far as to challenge Krissy's wishes and become Bryan's guardian in Paige's place was unconscionable.

"Apparently this case is a little more complicated than I had anticipated." Swiveling his chair, Judge Willinger talked quietly to his court clerk. After a moment, he returned his attention to Paige and the others.

"I believe this young man will be best served if I refer the case to a mediator. Because you, Miss Barclay, and you, Mr. Red Elk, both care about the boy, you'll be able to work out Bryan's living arrangement."

Bryan jumped to his feet. "I'm not going to move to Seattle with Aunt Paige! I won't go!"

"Sit down, son," the judge said patiently. "In two years, when you're fourteen, under Montana law you'll be able to decide where to live. But for now, promise me you'll let the adults work this out."

Bryan sat, but his red-faced expression spoke more loudly than any words could. He wasn't promising any such thing.

Sick at heart, Paige squeezed her eyes closed. How could her plans, Krissy's wishes, the thing her parents would have wanted, have gone so wrong?

The court clerk finished her telephone conversation and whispered something to the judge.

He nodded and turned back to Paige and the others. "Your appointment with the mediator is scheduled for next Wednesday at 10:00 a.m. here at the courthouse. Meanwhile, Mr. Red Elk, you'll need to complete the necessary paperwork to contest Miss Barclay's application."

The judge stood and swept out of the room, the court stenographer right behind him.

Paige's hopes and dreams for her future as Bryan's guardian, the chance to raise him, to love him as her own, shimmered like a desert mirage. Insubstantial.

As empty as her own life had been.

What would she do if the mediator recommended Jay as guardian instead of her?

Chapter Twelve

"I'm sorry, Paige."

Stepping out of the courthouse side by side, Bryan running ahead of them toward the parking lot, Paige angled a look at Jay. "No. You are not sorry. You softened me up. Made me care. And then undermined my application to be Bryan's guardian."

"I was afraid Bryan might do something crazy."

"Like actually want to move to Seattle?"

She climbed into the truck. Bryan was already in the backseat, avoiding her gaze. Head held high, she stared out the window. She was sure of one thing. No matter what happened with the mediator, she'd never again trust Jay.

Although Paige had no appetite, Jay stopped at a drive-thru to pick up lunch before they left Kalispell. They ate as he drove them back to Bear Lake.

They didn't speak.

The countryside on the outskirts of Kalispell spread out flatter than the area around Bear Lake, much of it planted with cherry orchards. Scattered fruit stands stood empty waiting for the harvest.

What would she do if she and Jay couldn't come to terms and the mediator ruled against her?

She drew a painful breath. She had her job. Her career. *If* she didn't get fired for staying away too long. For trying to do what she thought was best for Bryan.

Was she wrong? Had Krissy and Grandpa been wrong?

It's what Mom and Dad would want you to do.

She glanced at her watch as Jay turned off the highway, following the red arrow on the Bear Lake Outfitters sign. He pulled the truck up in front of the main house. Bryan started to get out.

"Wait just a minute," she said, trying to stop Bryan. "I'm going to Seattle for the weekend. There's a big conference scheduled and my boss really wants me there by tomorrow when the guests start checking into the hotel. I'd like you to come with me, Bryan."

"Tomorrow's the last day of school." He pushed his door all the way open.

"You'd have free run of the hotel. There's a heated swimming pool. An exercise room. Even a rec room with table tennis and darts. Cable TV. I'll bring you back home on Monday."

"I'd rather stay here." He hopped down from the truck.

"If you come along, you'd get a chance to see my condo and a little of the city. Of course, I'm planning to buy a larger condo if you—"

"I'm not gonna live in a condo. Not ever."

"Then a house. We can find something—" She heard the desperation in her voice, but it was too late. He'd already run off toward the barn and stables. His horse and the dog. His favorite things that she could never give him.

Tears clogged her throat. If he'd just give her a chance, they could be happy in Seattle.

An hour later, Jay was in the barn office doing some paperwork when Henry came shuffling in. "Paige left for Seattle. She seemed pretty upset."

"I know." Jay was wound up fairly tight, too. From the moment he'd told the judge he wanted to be Bryan's guardian, Paige had looked like she'd been run over by a herd of wild horses. She'd never seen it coming. He hadn't meant to blindside her. Guilt zinged him with a headache, a shot right between the eyes. But he had tried to tell her Seattle wasn't going to work for Bryan.

Henry pulled up another chair, dusted the seat off with his hat and sat down. "You want to tell me what's going on? All Paige said was that she'd be back next week for another hearing." He smoothed the brim of his hat before putting it back on.

"I think I messed up big time, but I didn't know what else to do." Jay told him about the court hearing, how he'd signed up to be Bryan's guardian and how there would be another meeting to mediate the case.

"Why'd you go and do a fool thing like that?" Henry scrunched his face, his wrinkles folding into a troubled mask.

"Because of the kid. Bryan's threatening to run away."

"Nonsense. Once he knows he has to move to Seattle, he'll settle down."

"I don't think so, Henry. He seems dead serious to me." Bryan had ridden out of here as soon as he could after they'd gotten back home. He hadn't even taken time to change out of his good jeans. Jay had made sure the boy hadn't packed any gear to take with him. He was just out for a ride. Blowing off steam.

Removing his hat again, Henry scratched the top of his balding head. "I thought you and Paige were getting along pretty good."

"We were." But not anymore. Jay tripping her up had seen to that.

"I love that girl, son. You, too. Was kind of hoping there'd be a spark between you."

"Yeah, there's a spark but it can't start much of a fire if she's living in Seattle and I'm living here."

Henry settled his hat back on his head and stood. "Pity there isn't a way to fix that." Moving slowly, he walked out of the office.

Staring after the old man, Jay knew he didn't want to move to Seattle any more than Bryan did. The only difference was that Jay was an adult. He couldn't be forced to live somewhere else.

Neither could Paige.

A real pity. Because he'd like a little more time to see if that *spark* Henry was talking about could ignite a full-fledged wildfire.

Driving straight through for nine hours got Paige home after midnight.

Her eyes burning from staring into headlights and her back aching, she hauled her suitcase upstairs and collapsed on her bed. She dragged the pillow into her arms, curled around it and cried the tears she'd been holding back all the way from Bear Lake.

When she woke, she staggered into the bathroom to take a shower. One look in the mirror and she knew there wasn't enough makeup in the world to disguise her puffy eyes.

If Jay hadn't kissed her, his betrayal wouldn't hurt so much. Why couldn't he have told her from the beginning that he wanted to be Bryan's guardian? At least she would have been prepared for a battle.

As she drank her coffee, she walked through her condo. She'd gone for contemporary furniture with smooth, simple lines and pastel colors in the living room. Oddly, after her time at Grandpa's house, it all looked dainty, not at all suitable for a big man like Jay. Or even an active boy like Bryan.

No stains on the carpet. No clutter on the coffee table. No comfortable spot for a twelve-year-old boy to sprawl out and be himself.

Of course, with her work schedule, she wasn't home often enough to make a mess. If Bryan lived here, she'd make it a point to be home more often. To spend quality time with him.

She winced as she stepped into her home office. A desk, chair and filing cabinet filled most of the room. She'd have to move most of it out into the living room to make space for Bryan, even temporarily.

If she could get him to Seattle. Compared to the wide open spaces of Montana, he'd hate living here.

She pulled her lip between her teeth. She'd make it better for him. She vowed she would. *If* he gave her a chance.

She dressed in a green silk suit she had bought off the sale rack at Nordstrom. Picking up her briefcase and laptop, she went downstairs to her car. She didn't know many of her neighbors except for Mrs. Martell, an older woman who sometimes asked Paige to come in to feed her cats when she was away. Mrs. Martell had also been the one to invite her to church shortly after Paige had moved into the condo complex, which had been a true blessing.

As far as Paige knew, no children lived in this condo complex at all. Strictly an adult crowd.

Not much fun for a kid like Bryan.

The Elite Hotel in Seattle was fifteen stories tall and boasted a ballroom that seated nine hundred, if you squeezed them in tightly enough.

Paige used her employee pass to enter the underground garage. She wound her way down to the lowest level, parked and rode the elevator to the lobby. The buzz of guests chatting in various conversational groups greeted her as she stepped out onto the granite floor.

Compared to the silence surrounding her grandfather's house, the noise generated by these strangers offended her auditory nerves.

She waved a greeting to the bell captain and turned down the hallway to the guest services offices.

A stack of unopened mail overflowed her in-basket. A jumble of pink phone-message notes covered the top of her desk.

She scooped up the messages and sat down. Sorting through the pink slips, she discovered several from Mr. Emerald, her contact with the innkeepers' association. Apparently he'd been asking for changes in the original conference plan. Nowhere on the note had Betsy indicated she had taken care of the request. Paige was going to have to backtrack—

Mr. Armstrong rushed into her office. Usually he was very calm, almost staid, but today his face was flushed, his perfect silver hair mussed and his eyes wild.

"That Emerald fellow is demanding a wine cocktail reception tonight." His highbrow English accent had turned Cockney. "Seven o'clock. He claims he called about it but no one got back to him."

Entirely possible given the pink message slips on Paige's desk. "Apparently Betsy wasn't able to return his calls. Does catering know about the change?"

"They do not! You need to fix this right away. Peter is going to have a fit and Emerald is stomping all over the hotel complaining to anyone who'll listen what a mistake it was to book their conference here."

"Yes, sir. I'll be happy to talk to them both immediately." Of course, Mr. Armstrong was perfectly capable of altering the arrangements, but he'd rather yell at her.

"I can't imagine what made you think you could take two weeks off, Ms. Barclay. Not during our busy season."

"Yes, it was unfortunate timing that my sister

died so unexpectedly." It was always busy season at the Seattle Elite Hotel.

Her sarcastic comment silenced him for a moment. Then he recovered as though she hadn't spoken and fussed at her about other details. When his tirade slowed, she asked, "Where might I find Mr. Emerald?"

"In the lobby. You can't miss him. He looks like a bowling ball in a Hawaiian shirt. That's the theme he wants for the cocktail party."

Great! She had to put a theme cocktail party together, including appropriate hors d'oeuvres and decorations, in seven hours. Peter Smedley, the catering manager, was going to kill her.

As predicted, Mr. Emerald was easy to spot. Unfortunately, he'd drawn a crowd of innkeepers around him, and he was waxing on about the lousy service they were getting.

Putting on her cheerful, competent face, Paige walked up to him and introduced herself. "I am so sorry there has been some miscommunication about this evening's cocktail party. If you'd like to step over to reception, I'm sure we can accommodate the changes you asked for."

As he blustered about everything that was wrong, Paige couldn't help but imagine Mr. Emerald doing the hula in his garish shirt, rotating his ample figure to ukulele music. Only half listening to Emerald's complaints, she smiled as the "Hawaiian Wedding Song" played in her head.

When Emerald finally ran out of grievances, she agreed to make everything right for him, and quickly gave him a new estimate of cost. After a little sputtering, he signed the addendum to the contract.

Heading off to find Peter in catering, she mused that Jay, who was so athletic and physically graceful, would be a much better hula dancer than Mr. Emerald.

Jay would probably insist he would never do the hula; it was too girlie for a tough wrangler. And the image that came to mind was one she did not need and she forced it aside.

Why in the world was she thinking about Jay anyway? She'd wanted him to be her ally. He'd chosen to oppose her.

Bringing his trail riders back from an all-day trip through national forest land, Jay led them to the corral where they could dismount. He almost expected to see Paige standing on the front porch, a soft, gentle smile of welcome on her face.

But no, she wasn't there. She might never smile at him again.

He'd seen a bald eagle in flight around noon today and thought of Paige. She'd been so wide-eyed. Eager for the sights Mother Nature provided.

She'd shared his awe at the natural cathedral where he'd kissed her.

He wondered if she was just as eager in her hotel job. Probably. When she set her mind to something, she was fully committed, whether it was learning to ride a horse or being Bryan's guardian.

Picturing her hobnobbing with fancy business-men in their suits and ties, he felt her absence like a physical blow to his midsection.

Bryan came running out of the barn. "I'll unsad-dle the horses and get 'em cooled down."

"Great." He relinquished the reins to the boy. "How was the last day of school?"

"Okay, I guess. Mrs. Waterfield said I'd be in Mr. King's sixth grade class next year."

If Bryan was still living in Bear Lake.

"He's a cool dude," Bryan continued. "At recess he comes out and plays basketball with the guys."

"Sounds like you'd like having him for a teacher."

"Yep. Can I go on the trail ride tomorrow?"

"Sure. If Henry says you can."

Bryan tugged on the reins, taking the two horses to their respective stalls.

If Paige had her way, tomorrow's trail ride might be the last Bryan took for a long time. Unless the boy made good on his threat and went riding off on his own.

Removing his hat, Jay threaded his fingers through his hair. *Please God, whatever happens, watch over Bryan and keep him safe. Especially if You decide he should live in Seattle with Paige.*

Somehow, in the past five years Bryan had become the son he was never likely to have. He didn't want to go through the heartbreak of losing a second son.

Jay's guts twisted as he went to round up the rest of the horses to be unsaddled, fed and groomed. When it came to Bryan's future, it was really hard to say *Thy will be done.*

Paige's neighbor, Mrs. Martell, called her Sunday morning inviting her to go to the early service at church.

On the short drive to the church on the corner, Paige brought her up-to-date about her trip to Bear Lake and the complications she'd encountered.

"How wonderful it is that you've taken responsibility for the young boy. I'm sure you'll be an incredible guardian for him." Mrs. Martell always wore gloves and a hat to church, usually a small one that perched on top of her gray hair. A stylish throwback to an earlier era.

"I hope so. But I'm going to have to move. My condo is way too small for two." Paige had dressed in a navy power suit to go to work after she dropped Mrs. Martell at home following the church service.

"Oh, dear, I'll miss having you for a neighbor. But I'm sure it's for the best. God must have something special in mind for you, you're such a good person. He'll lead you on the right path."

Paige wasn't sure about being a 'good person,' not after some of the diabolical thoughts she'd contemplated to get revenge on Mr. Emerald. But she could hope that the Lord would have a hand in leading her on His chosen path.

Chapter Thirteen

Paige left Seattle at a civilized hour on Monday morning. Her boss hadn't been pleased she was returning to Bear Lake so soon. After the weekend babysitting several hundred innkeepers, she didn't much care what Mr. Armstrong thought.

She stopped in Missoula at a grocery store and picked up some barbecue ribs she could reheat for dinner, a big tub of coleslaw and one of potato salad. Maybe the way to the heart of a growing boy like Bryan was via his stomach.

As she drove north on Highway 93 through Polson, her anxiety grew. She'd been so hurt by Jay challenging her request for guardianship, she didn't know what to say to him. If anything.

What must Bryan be thinking at this point? Maybe during her absence, he had calmed down a little. Adjusted to the idea of moving to Seattle.

Her mouth dry, an ache in her chest, she pulled

up in front of her grandfather's house. Almost immediately Grandpa appeared on the front porch. He waved and smiled.

"There you are, child. How'd it go in Seattle?"

"About as expected. Demanding guests and crazed staff." Opening the door, she climbed out of the car. She inhaled the sweet scent of pine trees and fresh mountain air. Too bad she couldn't bottle enough to fill her condo with the invigorating perfume.

He came down the steps and hugged her. "Good to have you back, child. I missed you."

"I missed you too, Grandpa." He felt wiry and tough, his cheeks rough with a day's growth of whiskers. "How did your doctor appointment go?"

"That youngster said I was fit as can be."

She raised her brows.

"I have to keep taking those silly pills. Waste of money." He *harrumphed*. "Well, bring your things on in. You know where to put them."

"I brought dinner. Barbecued spare ribs." Smiling at her grandfather's attitude, she opened the car's back door and retrieved the grocery sacks. When she turned around, Jay was standing right in front of her. His broad shoulders were rigid, as if he expected to be attacked, his blue-green eyes beneath the brim of his cowboy hat unreadable.

Even so, with his chiseled cheekbones and strong jaw, he was the most potent male she'd ever known.

So much more of a man's man than any of those innkeepers and the Mr. Armstrongs of the world, he nearly took her breath away.

"I'll carry those in for you," he said.

"Thanks." As she passed the groceries to him, their hands brushed. An electric pulse shot up her arm. How could she have forgotten what an impact he had on her? Why hadn't she gotten over him while she was in Seattle?

It would take more than three days to achieve that much amnesia.

From the trunk, she retrieved her suitcase. This time she'd brought along her own jeans and more casual clothes, including her running shoes.

She put her suitcase in the sewing room and went to the kitchen to put away the groceries. Jay was examining the wrapped barbecue ribs.

"I'll reheat those in the microwave for dinner," she said.

"Great." His gaze skimmed over her. "I like your jeans."

"Krissy's didn't fit me right."

"Krissy was different than you are in a lot of ways."

"Yes, she was."

"I don't think she ever fixed barbecue ribs."

Paige looked at the way Jay was cradling the ribs in his big hands. "Reheating something isn't that hard to do."

"For some people it can be. Especially if they got it wrong the first time."

Wondering what Jay's sudden fascination with ribs was all about, she took them to put in the refrigerator along with the coleslaw and potato salad. Then she washed the apples and oranges she'd bought and put them on the counter to drain. There had been some cherries on sale but the price was still too high. Another few weeks and the local cherries would be in the stores.

"Everything go okay in Seattle?" he asked.

"The usual crush of problems. Nothing I couldn't handle." Why was he just standing there leaning against the counter? Wasn't there a horse that needed grooming or something?

"I'm sure you're good at your job."

Then why didn't he think she'd be a good guardian for Bryan? She had to "mother" the hotel guests 24/7. Even spoil them if that's what was needed to get their return business. How much harder could a twelve-year-old be to raise?

"If I stay away much longer, I won't have a job."

"So you'll be going back right after the mediation meeting?"

She turned to face him straight on. "With or without Bryan, I'll go back to Seattle after the hearing. That's where my life is, Jay."

"And Bryan's life and mine are here." His liquid voice held a river of pain. "I'll see you at dinner."

He walked out through the mudroom, the back door slamming behind him.

She covered her mouth with her hand. She was *not* going to cry over a man who had betrayed her. She was through with that. Now she was going to move on with her life.

One way or another.

The following morning, Paige rounded up the bags of Krissy's clothing and personal items to take to the Second Time Around thrift shop.

A wave of grief nearly undid her as she put the last bag in the trunk of her car. Krissy would only be a memory now. Her pictures in scrapbooks the only tangible evidence of her life.

Her pictures and her son.

Somehow Paige would have to keep Krissy's memory alive for Bryan.

After delivering Krissy's things to the thrift shop, Paige's next stop was the local branch of Lake Country Bank in Bear Lake to determine how to transfer Krissy's accounts into a trust for Bryan at her bank in Seattle.

She made one last stop at the Love 2 Read Books and Bakery. Given the stress of dealing with Krissy's final affairs, and Mr. Emerald in Seattle, she deserved a sugary treat.

The interior of the shop was as cute and quaint as the exterior caricature of a baker reading a book on the large picture window. Several glass-topped vintage ice cream tables and chairs with wire backs twisted into a heart shape were scattered about. One entire wall was filled with bookshelves displaying mostly paperback books for sale. From the covers, it looked like more than half were romance novels.

Wrinkling her nose, Paige decided she wasn't likely to have the same happy ending with Jay that the heroines in those books achieved.

Standing in front of the bakery display case, she inhaled the scent of cinnamon, fresh-baked bread, chocolate and apple. Her mouth watered.

"Can I help you?" A high-school-aged girl greeted her with a smile from behind the counter. She wore a pale pink bib apron with the same caricature of a baker reading a book on the front that was on the window.

"I'd like a dozen assorted bear claws to go." Surely they would appeal to Bryan's sweet tooth in the morning. "And I'll take one of the double chocolate chewy cookies to have now."

"Yes, ma'am, those cookies are our most popular." The girl boxed up the bear claws, handed her the cookie on a napkin and rang up the order on the cash register.

As soon as Paige got in her car, she took a bite of the cookie. Oversize chocolate chips and creamy dark chocolate melted in her mouth and tantalized her taste buds. She feared this one cookie alone would add an inch to her thighs.

Right now, she didn't even care.

The only time Paige saw either Jay or Bryan that day was at mealtime. She wasn't able to entice Bryan into playing the piano or even a video game with her after dinner. When she started a conversation with him, all she got in return was a grunt.

She woke Wednesday morning with a dull headache that throbbed at the back of her skull. The muscles in her shoulders and back felt like they'd been twisted into a pretzel.

From the empty bakery box, she concluded the men of the household had made quick work of the bear claws she'd bought in town.

Although she would have preferred to drive her own car to Kalispell for the custody mediation, Jay insisted all of them—including Grandpa, who demanded he go along this time—would be more comfortable in his extended cab truck. Since Grandpa had been feeling much stronger, and he had a stake in Bryan's future, Paige couldn't object to his demand.

She sat in the backseat with Bryan, who scrunched himself into the far corner. Her heart ached with the hope that the boy would *want* to live with her, but she'd feared that battle had already been lost. Perhaps permanently.

"You know all of us are trying to do the right thing for you," she told Bryan.

He kept his eyes glued on the passing scenery. "It isn't right that somebody can make me move to Seattle."

"If that's how the mediator rules, I'd like for you to at least give it a try. It's what your mother wanted."

He didn't respond. Instead he kept staring out the window. The wall he'd erected between himself and Paige seemed impenetrable. If anything, he was more determined than ever not to accept Paige as his guardian.

It pained Paige the most that Jay had sided with the boy against her. If only he had supported her efforts, maybe Bryan would have willingly agreed to the move.

At the courthouse, they were directed to a conference room with a large table in the center and chairs on both sides. Grandpa sat beside Paige. Jay and Bryan sat opposite them. A perfect picture of a family in conflict.

Paige retrieved the paperwork from her briefcase and placed it on the table in front of her. While they waited, anxiety and fear filled the silent room like a foggy day on Puget Sound. The dampness chilled her.

Paige remembered dark nights when her childish fears became living things, ugly green monsters hiding under the bed. She'd wanted to call her mother to come hold her. But her mother worked hard all day. Paige knew not to disturb her mother's sleep. If only the monsters would leave Paige alone.

She started when the conference room door opened, admitting a tall woman who resembled a gray-haired scarecrow with a particularly prominent nose.

"Sorry to keep you waiting. I'm Angela Quinn," she said, introducing herself in a pleasant, well-modulated tone. She sat at the head of the table and opened a file folder. "In my experience, disputes regarding guardianship can be among the most stressful, so let's all see if we can keep our emotions under control. For young Bryan's sake, if nothing else."

She directed her attention to Bryan. "First of all, I want you to know how sorry I am that you lost your mother." She spoke directly to him as though there was no one else in the room. "That's a hard thing to deal with at any age. How are you doing?"

He shrugged, typical-adolescent style. "I'm okay."

"Good. I hope you know you're fortunate that two people love you enough that they want to be your guardian."

He cut Paige a glance and immediately lowered his gaze.

Paige felt sorry for the poor kid. He hadn't asked

to be orphaned. Or to have the aunt he barely knew be chosen by his mother to take care of him after she died.

Ms. Quinn turned to Paige. "I take it you're willing to be Bryan's guardian, Miss Barclay."

"Yes, ma'am. Although I was surprised at first, I'm honored that my sister named me in her will. I'm very eager to serve as Bryan's guardian."

A tiny frown lowered Ms. Quinn's brows. "Why were you surprised?"

Paige realized she'd dug herself into a hole. "Well, I hadn't thought… My sister was so young, I hadn't given any thought to what might happen if Krissy… Kristine died."

Ms. Quinn nodded. "I see. And you, Mr. Red Elk? Is there a particular reason why you are contesting Miss Barclay's appointment? Do you find her unsuitable for the task?"

"No, ma'am." Bryan started to say something, but Jay stopped him by putting his hand on the boy's arm. "Miss Barclay is a fine woman. Certainly she's well intentioned. But she lives in Seattle and plans to move Bryan there to live with her. I believe Bryan would be better off to stay where he is, living with his great-grandfather, Henry Stephenson, and me." Jay indicated Grandpa. "It's the only home he's ever known."

"I take it you are Mr. Stephenson's employee?"

"Yes, ma'am. I've worked for him at the Bear Lake Outfitters for five years now."

"And you, Mr. Stephenson. What is your opinion in this matter?"

"I love the boy. His grandmother and I helped raise him since he was born." He patted Paige's arm. "I love my granddaughter, too. Bryan's mother picked Paige herself. As much as I'd like for Bryan to stay with me, I have to believe Krissy knew what she was doing. I'm getting up in years now and won't be around much longer."

Paige bit the inside of her cheek. Taking Bryan away from Grandpa would leave him all alone. Except for Jay. Had Krissy realized what that would do to their grandfather? Had Paige seriously taken that into account?

Second thoughts tumbled through her head. She wanted so much to be a parent to Bryan. A fill-in mother, who she hoped he would learn to love.

Wasn't this what her parents would have expected of her?

"Generally speaking," Ms. Quinn said, "in the absence of any evidence of incapacity or cause to believe possible harm would come to the child, we try to comply with the wishes of the deceased parent."

"No!" Bryan jumped to his feet.

Grabbing the tail of Bryan's shirt, Jay tugged him back down.

"Bryan, I know this is hard for you to understand."

The mediator's pale eyes filled with sympathy. "Your aunt does love you. Given the facts that Mr. Red Elk is not a relative and Mr. Barclay is in support of his granddaughter, it would be very difficult for me to make any other recommendation. You will be notified when Judge Willinger's decision is recorded."

Bryan laid his head down on his arms. His slender, young body shook with silent sobs.

Paige looked across the table at Jay. He held her gaze for a moment before trying to console Bryan.

Swallowing hard, Paige tried to halt the stinging tears of joy that she had been chosen and the bitter taste of the cost her nephew was paying.

Clearly there was no winner here.

Clouds in the evening sky blocked the rising moon when Jay went out to the barn to find Bryan. He hadn't spoken on the way home in the truck and hadn't come in for dinner. Usually the kid had a hollow leg. Missing meals was a bad sign.

He was relieved Bright Star still stood in his stall. So far Bryan hadn't acted on his threat. The kid sat on the floor, his back braced against the wall. Archie whined and her tail lifted in greeting as Jay sat down next to the boy.

"Tough day, huh?" Jay handed Bryan a chicken sandwich.

"I guess." He unwrapped the sandwich, took a bite and set it aside.

Archie sniffed the chicken. Jay pushed the dog's nose away, ordering her to leave it.

With Bright Star eyeing them, they all sat in silence for a time.

"I've been thinking," Jay finally said. "Maybe we could talk your Aunt Paige into letting you stay here for the summer. I can sure use you on trail rides and helping with the horses." He'd seen how conflicted Paige had been when the mediator had made her decision and as she saw Bryan's reaction. Maybe now she'd recognize the need to give the boy a little more time before taking him to Seattle.

"She won't change her mind." Bryan's sullen tone matched his sour expression.

"We could ask her."

"Wouldn't make any difference."

Jay took off his hat and leaned his head back against the stall wall. He admitted Paige could be stubborn. And determined. But he didn't think she wanted to intentionally hurt Bryan. Even if Jay thought what Paige was doing was wrong, she believed it was right.

Maybe she was doing exactly what God had in mind for Bryan. Jay couldn't be the judge. He'd have to accept it. Even if he wished down deep in his soul that the answer was different. That Bryan stayed here in Bear Lake.

And that Paige did, too.

Jay had had trouble keeping his faith in the Lord

when Annie and their unborn son had died. He'd struggled hard. In time he'd come to realize that while he'd never understand why God had taken them from him, the Lord knew and understood his pain.

Jay would have to have faith again that whatever happened, the Lord's guiding hand was with him.

In her room after dinner, Paige asked the Lord to help her reach out to Bryan, to make him understand she wasn't the enemy. The boy had skipped dinner. And when later he still hadn't come in the house, Jay went out to check on him.

Jay had made it abundantly clear Bryan wouldn't want to talk to her tonight. Maybe not ever.

As she searched for answers in the Bible, she found many passages about God's love for His children. Was her love for Bryan as righteous as God's love? Or had her decision to be Bryan's guardian been the selfish act of a willful woman? A woman whose need for love had blinded her to a child's needs.

The bitter, condemning truth rang in her ears. *You have no right to take Bryan away from all he loves.*

Her chin trembled. Bryan was a child of light and day, of forests and canyons, of God's earth. She could not transplant him to a foreign place of sidewalks and high-rises and expect him to thrive.

Bowing her head, she made the only decision she could. The one the Lord would want her to make.

Paige strained to hear Bryan return to the house, his footsteps in the hallway. Should she go out the barn to look for him?

When at last she heard him pass her door, she sighed with relief. But he made no effort to stop to talk with her. Tomorrow would be soon enough to tell him she'd changed her mind; he could stay with Jay and Grandpa. Bryan's happiness was more important than hers.

Drained of hope, she fell into an exhausted sleep with tears edging down her cheeks and the Bible still in her lap.

She dreamed that Jesus showed the many rooms in His Father's house. Oddly, they all looked like rooms in a rustic hotel with paintings of mountains on the pinewood walls and table lamps made out of deer antlers.

Heavy footsteps startled her awake. Then she heard Jay's voice. "Bryan's taken Bright Star. They're both gone."

Grandpa mumbled a response at the same time Paige struggled to her feet, trying to shake the dream from her mind. *Bryan gone?* How could that be? She had thought there would be time to talk.

With no thought that she was wearing only a nightgown and her feet were bare, she yanked the sewing room door open. She hurried down the hallway to Bryan's room and switched on the light. The lump of blankets on the bed gave her a brief shot of relief until she realized the lump wasn't Bryan. Beneath the blankets there was nothing but a pillow.

Thinking, praying, that it was a childish prank, a way to punish her, she whirled around. Looked in the closet. Peered under the bed. He couldn't be gone! He was just a child. Yes, he'd threatened to run away. She hadn't believed he actually would. Not when it came right down to it; she had been sure he'd come with her to Seattle.

But this was no joke.

Her decision had come too late.

She raced to the kitchen where she heard Jay and Grandpa talking. She found them in the mudroom standing by the gun cabinet, Grandpa in his flannel pajamas, Jay dressed in old jeans and an unbuttoned shirt, both his clothes and his hair wet from the rain.

Her eyes widened with fear and horror when she saw the lock on the cabinet door hanging open. "What's going on? Where's Bryan?"

The weathered lines of Grandpa's aging face seemed to have collapsed downward. "He's gone. He took a hunting rifle with him and some ammo."

The accusation in Jay's eyes burned her with its intensity. "I was afraid he'd make good on his threat. It started to rain around four o'clock. I woke up and went to check that the stable was shut up tight. He'd locked Archie in the tack room and took Bright Star."

"How long has he been gone?" Her knees trembled. Grasping the doorjamb, she steadied herself. Guilt burrowed its way deep inside her. This was *her* fault. If only she'd told him her decision when he'd come in to bed.

Jay hefted a rifle from the cabinet and worked the mechanism. "I have no idea when he left. I sent him inside earlier. Figured he'd go to bed."

"I heard him come in," Paige said.

"I did, too," Grandpa agreed.

"He's not here now. I looked. He'd piled up his blankets and pillow to make it look like he was sleeping."

"See if he took any food with him," Jay ordered. "Henry, check the camping and fishing gear. He might've taken that along, too."

Frantically, Paige jerked open the cabinets. A nearly full jar of peanut butter was gone. The box of granola bars was missing. A loaf of bread. Cans of soup. In the refrigerator the shelf where the milk was stored was empty.

"He's taken enough food to last a day or two," Paige reported.

Grandpa returned to the kitchen. His pale face made him look like he'd aged ten years in the past half hour.

"The boy's got his fishing gear with him and a bedroll. He's planning to stay out there a while."

Jay hooked his hand around the back of his neck. "He's planning to live off the land."

"He can't do that," Paige cried. "He's just a little boy. And the weather...you have to go after him. Bring him home."

"I will." The rifle still in his hand, Jay shut the gun cabinet door. "I can't track him in the dark. I'll leave at first light."

"That'll give him too much of a lead. You won't be able to catch him," she protested.

"Don't worry. I'll find him."

But how long would Bryan be out there on his own? This was her fault. She had to do something.

"I'm going with you," she said.

Glaring at her, Jay said, "Don't be ridiculous."

"Jay will find him for us," Grandpa said.

"That may well be," Paige said. "But Bryan is so upset, I'm not sure he'll come back with Jay unless he knows for sure, hears it with his own ears, that I'm not going to make him move to Seattle."

Jay's mouth gaped open. Grandpa cleared his throat.

Before they could say anything, she left them standing there and rushed back to the sewing room. She could barely draw a breath. Her chest felt like it was about to explode. She would never have a chance to form a small but loving family with Bryan.

He didn't want her.

She should have known she couldn't force someone to love her. No matter how good an aunt she tried to be.

Or a daughter.

Only her self-absorption with her own desires had made her believe otherwise.

Chapter Fourteen

With the sun just peeping through the clouds over the eastern mountains, Jay tightened the cinch on Thunder Boy's saddle, then hefted saddle bags filled with trail mix and emergency rations into place.

He turned to see Paige struggling to saddle Peaches. He grimaced. *Fool woman!*

"Once I pick up Bryan's trail, I'm going to be traveling fast," he told her. "You won't be able to keep up."

"I'll keep up." Wearing Henry's floppy hat and a poncho over her jacket, she righted the saddle. She grappled under the horse to find the cinch. Henry had loaned her some gloves, too. She'd need them before this was over.

"It may take all day to catch up with him. You've never ridden more than two hours at a time. If you fall back, I'll have to leave you on your own," he threatened.

Henry helped her settle her saddlebags on the horse and snugged a bedroll wrapped in oil cloth down tight.

"Don't you worry about me. I won't slow you down."

Of course she would. And he couldn't leave on her own, not with mountain lions and bears prowling the area. She'd be defenseless.

"I know you feel this is your fault—"

"It is my fault. I'm going to make it right."

Even if it kills me.

Jay tied his bedroll to the back of his saddle. No telling how long they'd be out in the weather. He could feel the temperature dropping already. It wasn't unheard of to get snow in the higher elevations in late May or even early June.

He slid his rifle into its scabbard.

If Bryan hadn't been so cocky about living off the land, if he hadn't been as determined and as stubborn as his aunt, Jay wouldn't be going off after him into what could be turning into a serious storm. He could've stayed home, sat by the fire.

Enjoyed Paige's company.

Ha! That was a laugh. He'd blown that possibility when he had asked to be Bryan's guardian.

Henry helped boost Paige into the saddle.

Mounting Thunder Boy, Jay adjusted his rain slicker to cover himself as best he could. "Stay inside the corral. I'm going to take a look, see if I can spot Bryan's trail." The rain that had been fall-ing wasn't going to help. In low spots Bright Star's hoofprints were likely to be washed out.

"If you leave without me, I'll just follow you," Paige warned.

Yeah, Jay didn't doubt that for a minute. She didn't have the good sense of a spider to get in out of the rain. Plenty of spunk, though.

He opened the corral gate and walked Thunder Boy out. He kept his eyes on the ground. He figured Bryan was most likely heading to the lake where they'd taken the fishermen on Saturday. There'd been a lot of fish caught. Easy pickings is what Bryan would think.

Man, that felt like a thousand years ago.

But maybe Bryan would think that was too obvi-ous. That Jay would find him too easily. He could just as well have taken a different trail to throw Jay off. The kid was foolish to travel at night. Despite the boy's familiarity with all the trails in the area, in the dark it would be easy to get lost.

He patrolled the edge of the trail leading up the hill. Finally he spotted Bright Star's hoofprints. He could tell from the small cutout in the horse's left rear shoe.

He waved to Paige. "If you're coming, let's get a move on."

Once out of the corral gate, she heeled the horse up to a trot. She bounced like a rubber ball in the seat. At that pace, it was going to be a long day for her.

As she approached Jay, he turned his horse along the trail. He kept his eye on the ground as she came up behind him.

"We can go faster than this, can't we?" she asked.

"We could, but I might lose the trail."

Close in to the main house, several trails took off in various directions. Most weren't used much. But Bryan and he had ridden them all.

"Too bad Bryan doesn't have a cell phone," Paige said. "We could track his GPS."

"You've been watching too many big city police shows. In these mountains there's no cell coverage unless you have a satellite phone."

"I don't like crime shows. I watch PBS and Discovery."

"Ever see a show about Native Americans tracking their game?"

"I don't think so."

"You won't need to. Just watch me."

He heard an unladylike snort and smiled. At times he couldn't help but be amused by her determination when toughness was required. All five-feet-nothing-much of her could bristle like a mama bear protecting her cub.

The higher they went, the harder the rain fell. Visibility dropped to almost zero. They were inside the rain cloud itself.

He glanced behind him. "You still with me?"

"I'm here." Peaches plodded along following Thunder Boy, which is what she liked to do. Paige was hunkered inside her poncho as far as she could go.

"You can still go back. You could follow the trail home."

"Keep moving, cowboy," she said, her testy voice making it clear she wasn't going to quit. "Bryan's all alone. He could be scared or hurt. I can stick it out as long as you can."

She probably would, just to prove a point, he realized.

He came to a rocky section of the trail. Thunder Boy picked his way gingerly along the uneven path.

Behind him, he heard Peaches slip on a rock, followed by a cry of alarm. He turned in his saddle. "Are you okay?"

"I'm just dandy." She gripped the saddle horn with two hands.

Brave girl!

Paige decided this was the stupidest thing she'd ever done. She could barely see Jay ahead of her through the mist and rain. Peaches kept losing her footing on the slick rocks. On the edge of terror, Paige was sure both she and the horse would slide off the trail and down the hill at any moment.

Dumb! Dumb! Dumb!

But what else could she do? She couldn't passively just wait for Jay to bring Bryan home. Because she'd been so wrapped up in herself and what she needed, he'd run away. She hadn't been thinking about him. She hadn't listened to his pleas. She'd been deaf to what he needed.

Exactly like her own mother.

Tears filmed her eyes, making it even harder to see through the mist. She wiped them away with the back of her gloved hand.

She vowed that she would never again ignore a child's cry for help. Not with Bryan. Not with any child if she was ever blessed enough to have one of her own.

To her surprise, Jay reined his horse off the trail and under a stand of fir trees.

"What's wrong?" she asked, following him. "Have you lost Bryan's trail?"

"Nope." He dismounted. "The horses need a rest. So do you."

"I can keep going."

"Fine. But you'll have to walk. The horses come first."

He was right, of course. She pulled her feet from the stirrups to dismount and slid to the ground. When she landed, she couldn't prevent the groan that escaped. Her legs felt like she'd been doing splits for hours and they were stuck in that unnatural position.

"Walk around. That'll loosen your muscles." Jay led the horses to a spot where they could munch on some spring grass.

The layers of overlapping branches above Paige protected her from some of the rain. Still there was a steady *drip, drip* as drops ran off the tips of the tree branches, plopping onto the ground and on her head.

Jay handed her a granola bar and a steaming cup of coffee he'd poured from his thermos.

The coffee was almost hot enough to burn her tongue, but it felt wonderful as the liquid warmed her from the inside out.

"How far ahead of us do you think Bryan is?" she asked.

"Hard to tell. Bright Star's hoofprints have collected a lot of rainwater."

"Do you suppose he's smart enough to find some shelter to get in out of the rain?"

Jay looked off up the trail. "I don't know. Not many natural caves around here. A few rock overhangs. I taught him how to make a lean-to out of his poncho. That won't give him much shelter, but it would keep some of the rain off him and be a windbreak of sorts."

"If he stays out in this, he could catch pneumonia."

Jay took the empty cup from her and poured himself some coffee. "I'd say he's about as stubborn as his aunt is. He won't quit 'til he has to."

She twisted her lips into a frustrated grimace. She'd always thought of her determination as an asset, not a liability. She'd hate to think some of the same genes she carried were now putting her nephew at risk.

"Think you're ready to ride?" he asked.

"If Bryan can keep going, so can I."

She found her muscles weren't quite as willing to get back on the horse as her stubborn streak was. But Jay boosted her up. She grabbed the reins and the saddle horn.

"Let's ride," she said with more bravado than she felt.

Jay kept a close eye on the trail. He thought they were catching up with the boy. He'd seen one spot where Bryan had pulled off the trail to take a break. The poor kid had to be exhausted. Jay couldn't be sure when Bryan had sneaked his horse out of the stable—probably before it had started to rain. But he was confident Bryan hadn't gotten much sleep.

There was no sign that Bryan had turned off to the lake where they'd taken the fishermen. That worried Jay. The kid could be headed deep into the wilderness. Unlike some hiking trails in the national park, there were no shelters for hikers to get out of the weather on the route Bryan had chosen.

They'd ridden another half hour when Jay heard an ominous sound.

"What was that?" Paige asked.

Jay pulled his rifle from its scabbard. Worked back into position in his saddle. "Gunshot."

He dug his heels into Thunder Boy's ribs. This wasn't hunting season. Bryan had a gun. The shot had to have come from him. But why?

He'd find out soon enough. Though the way sounds echoed in a forest, he couldn't be sure, but he thought the shot hadn't come from too far away.

As the trail wound through trees and outcroppings of rock, he sent up a quick prayer. *Keep the boy safe, Lord.*

He heard a horse coming before he saw Bright Star barreling toward him at full gallop, saliva dripping from his mouth.

The saddle was empty.

"Whoa, boy! Whoa!" Jay tried to block Bright Star's frantic flight. He waved his arms. Reached for the flying reins. The terrified horse dodged past him.

"Stop him!" Paige cried.

Jay turned to see Paige nearly lose her seat lunging for Bright Star. She failed to catch the horse who raced past her, as well.

"Jay, what happened to Bryan? Why is his horse running like that?"

He watched Bright Star until he was out of sight. Chances were good the horse would make it back to the barn on his own. Nathan would take care of

im. Unless Bright Star fell and broke a leg before
e got home.

"I'll check on Bryan. You stay here." He reined
is horse up the trail. He didn't know what had
pooked Bright Star. Or why Bryan had taken a
hot at something. It had to mean trouble. He didn't
vant Paige caught in the middle.

A minute later, it didn't surprise him to hear
Peaches galloping up behind him. That woman was
ll grit and gumption. A man could learn to love
hat about her.

Alert to any possible danger, Jay carried his rifle
cross his saddle. He kept up a fast pace along the
rail as it twisted and turned through the woods.
When he reached an area where a forest fire had
corched the earth three years ago, he slowed. With
he trees burned to charcoal stumps, wildflowers
nd grass covered the landscape. Only a few pine
eedlings promised to return the scarred section to
forested hillside.

A great place for bears to forage, he thought.

"Bryan!" he called. "Can you hear me?"

He listened for a response. If anything, the rain
vas coming down harder now than it had before
nd was turning into big, fat drops that were being
lown around by an increasing wind. Forerunners
f snow if the temperature kept dropping.

He kept Thunder Boy moving at a steady pace.
"Bryan! Where are you?" The gunshot could mean

anything. That the kid had shot himself accidently. Or that the boy had encountered a mountain lion or a bear.

Jay called out again. "Bryan! We're coming."

At last he heard a faint reply. "Over here!"

That's my boy! "Stay where you are. I'll find you," he shouted.

"Did you hear him? Is he all right?" Paige's voice trembled, either with fear or excitement.

"We'll find out in a minute." Jay forged ahead, still watching the ground and keeping his eye on the surroundings.

Suddenly his blood turned icy cold. *Bear tracks.* Big ones.

He turned in his saddle to survey the area. He didn't want a bear to sneak up on them. Paige was lagging behind.

"You've gotta keep up with me," he ordered gruffly.

"I'm trying." Paige urged Peaches to pick up her pace.

Around the next bend, he spotted Bryan sitting under a tree. He held his rifle at the ready.

"We're here, son. You can put down the gun now." Dismounting, Jay dropped the reins to the ground knowing Thunder Boy would stay put. He walked toward the boy. Bryan's face was pale, his eyes wide. His hands holding the rifle shook.

Jay knelt beside him and gently took the rifle from him. "It's okay, son. You're going to be fine."

Suddenly Paige was kneeling beside him. "Bryan, honey, are you all right? We heard a shot."

"A b-bear. H-he was right on the t-trail. B-Bright Star spooked and threw me. My g-gun went off."

"Where's the bear now?" Jay asked.

"I dunno. He…took off…over the hill. I was…afraid he'd come back."

"Did you hit him? Is he wounded?" Jay really didn't need an injured bear raging through the woods.

"Naw. Bright Star reared…as I was trying to get off a shot."

"Just as well." Jay touched Paige's arm. "Get the bedroll and thermos from my horse. He's going into shock."

Paige dashed over to Jay's horse. Her hands were cold, her fingers uncoordinated. She struggled to undo the ties that held the bedroll in place, her ill-fitting gloves making the task even more difficult. This was her doing. Her fault that Bryan had been thrown from his horse.

When the bedroll finally came loose, she grabbed the thermos and rushed back to Bryan's side.

"Are you hurt?" she asked as Jay poured some coffee for the boy.

"My ankle. I t-twisted it. I couldn't get it out o the stirrup. I can't stand up."

Dear Lord in heaven. "I'm so sorry, Bryan," Paige said. "It's my fault you ran away. I didn't rec ognize how desperate you were. I was going to tel you this morning. But you were gone. I want you to be happy. If that means you staying here, then you'l stay." She gulped down a sob. She'd only known she was desperate to be his guardian, as her sis ter's final wish. To be loved by her sweet nephew "You don't have to move to Seattle. I promise I'l talk to the judge. Tell him you'd be better off with Jay and Grandpa."

"You'll do that?" Doubt turned his question into a prayer as he took the cup from Jay and sipped the warm liquid. He wrinkled his nose.

"I will. Just as soon as we can get you back home I promise." She knew her promise meant she'd have to return to Seattle, to her condo and her job, alone

She soothed her hand over Bryan's smooth cheek "I promise," she repeated, her throat constricted with the heartbreak of unfulfilled love and longing "But I'm going to come visit you. Often."

Slowly, as though he wasn't sure he could trust her, Bryan nodded. "Okay."

Jay examined the boy's ankle. "I can't tell much with your boot on, but I don't want to take it off 'm afraid it will swell up and we'll never get the ›oot back on."

He glanced around the open clearing. Only then lid Paige realize it had begun to snow. White flakes ıad begun to pile up against blackened tree stumps ınd in places sheltered from the wind.

"We need to get out of this weather and get Bryan varmed up before we start back. The horses need a est, too. I don't know how long this storm is going ›o last."

"What happened to Bright Star?" Bryan asked.

"He's probably already back at the barn," Jay said. 'He was moving pretty fast last time I saw him."

"Shouldn't we leave here in case the bear comes ›ack?" Paige's nerves were jangled enough. She lidn't need an angry bear charging at them from ›ut of nowhere.

"I don't think he will." Jay stood. "You stay here. 'm going to take a look around, see if there's a cave ›r someplace we can hang out for a while. Keep ʲour eyes open and yell if you see something."

"Something like a bear," Paige clarified.

"Yeah, something like that." He secured their ıorses then walked off through the trees.

Paige sat down next to Bryan and straightened ʰe bedroll that covered him. "If you're hungry, ʲe've got some trail mix and granola bars in the .addlebags."

"I'm okay." His color was better than when Paige had first seen him, which was a good sign.

Paige checked around for the bear. She hoped the gunshot had scared him off permanently.

"Are you real mad at me?" Bryan asked.

"No, honey. I'm not mad at you. Although running away wasn't the way to solve the problem. I'm mad at myself." Oddly, she wondered if leaving her family's home and moving to Seattle had been her way of running from her problems. And what of Jay selling his ranch and moving to Bear Lake? Had he been running away, too?

"How come you're upset with yourself?" Bryan asked.

"Because it was selfish of me to want you to move to Seattle when you obviously wanted to stay here."

He lifted one shoulder in an easy shrug. "Seattle might not have been so awful. I mean, you're not a bad person or anything."

She almost laughed. *Now* he decided it wouldn't be so bad. Leaning toward him, she kissed Bryan on the cheek. "Maybe you can come visit me someday."

"Can I still use the hotel pool and stuff?"

"Absolutely."

A branch cracked behind Paige in the woods. She spun around, exhaling a breath when she saw Jay in his yellow slicker returning.

"I found an overhang that looks deep enough to give us some cover," he said. "Let's lift Bryan up on Thunder Boy. It's too far for him to walk on that bad ankle."

Jay brought his horse closer. Together she and Jay got Bryan up on his good leg. He hopped a few steps, grabbed on to the saddle and Jay boosted him up.

Leading Peaches, Paige followed them down the hill through the trees until they reached the overhanging rock Jay had found. Over the years, wind and rain had hollowed out a six-foot-deep space. It didn't look like much of a shelter to Paige, but the ground was dry toward the back and the hillside blocked the worst of the wind.

"We'll get Bryan settled," Jay said, helping Bryan then unsaddling the horses. "I'm going to gather some wood for a fire."

"I feel like such a doofus," Bryan said as he lowered himself to the ground. "Messing up my ankle and stuff."

Paige tucked the bedroll around him. "Jay thinks you got your stubbornness from my genes."

"Really?" He laid down using Peaches's saddle for a headrest. Paige propped up his foot on a small boulder to keep the swelling minimized. "Mom could be pretty stubborn, too, if she wanted to do something and Grandpa didn't want her to."

"We came from the same gene pool." She smiled down at the boy and brushed his damp hair away from his forehead. "You rest now. It's been a long day for you."

For her, too, she thought as she sat down and leaned back against the rough wall of the cave. She closed her eyes.

Before she knew it, she felt the warmth of a fire on her chilled feet.

"You're back." She smiled at Jay, who was squatting down adding twigs to the fire he'd built.

"Back to two sleeping beauties."

She glanced at Bryan. "Poor kid. My selfishness sure did a number on him." He could have been killed or badly mauled by the bear. That, too, would have been her fault.

"You wanted to do the right thing."

"That's what I'm going to do as soon as we get back to Grandpa's house and I can talk to the family court judge."

"You're really going to give up the guardianship thing? Go back to Seattle without him?"

She pursed her lips to stop the denial that wanted to fly out of her mouth. Afraid to speak, she simply nodded.

He tipped his hat back and gazed at her with such intensity, it made her stomach churn.

"I wish there was a way you could stay here." His

voice was low and intimate, almost drowned out by the drumbeat of the rain.

Her heart echoed the same rhythm. She wished she could stay, too. But without a job…

Chapter Fifteen

Satisfied with the red coals glowing within the fire ring of stones he had gathered, Jay sat back and raised one knee, making himself comfortable.

From the beginning, he had fought Paige over Bryan's guardianship. Fought her in court. Now he wasn't so sure he'd done the right thing. After all, a boy needed a mother figure around to keep him on the straight and narrow.

And he'd hurt Paige. Badly.

Yeah, he still wanted Bryan to grow up right here in Bear Lake where he'd been born. That would be best for the boy.

But in the past couple weeks, Paige had made Jay feel things he hadn't felt since Annie was alive. Admiration. Pride in her accomplishments. And her determination.

Now Paige was going to leave. He knew the weight of loneliness that would follow.

He fed a few more twigs into the fire and watched the flames ignite. He couldn't have it both ways, keep Bryan here and Paige, too.

From the corner of his eye, he studied Paige. Wearing Henry's floppy hat, a poncho and old boots, she resembled a cowboy who had ridden hard across the prairie in a blizzard. But her cute little nose and her soft lips were totally feminine. Without a hint of makeup, her complexion was as rosy as a ripe peach hanging from a tree.

Yep, he was going to miss her. A lot.

"Guess you really like your job in Seattle," he said.

Sitting with her arms wrapped around her knees, she lifted her gaze from the fire to him. "Most days." Her voice held as much enthusiasm as a flat rock.

"Maybe when you get back to Seattle, you can talk Elite Hotels into building a four-star place here in Bear Lake. You could be the manager."

She choked out a quiet laugh that wouldn't wake Bryan. "That's not exactly their style. Although they do have a renovated nineteenth-century hunting lodge in the Lake District of northern England. Very elegant and posh."

"Bear Lake could use a little posh."

"Maybe." Even as she spoke, her gaze drifted away from him, her expression pensive.

"Had a guy on a trail ride here earlier this week.

He was pretty wiped out by the time we got back to the barn. Wished he didn't have to drive back to Kalispell to his ritzy hotel."

"I'm sure the B&Bs in Bear Lake are fine."

"Yeah, maybe, except his wife hadn't booked one. None of them are four stars."

Hooking one arm around his raised knee, he returned his attention to the fire. Even if he asked her to stay, what could he offer her? He was a hired hand. That's it. Granted he felt close to Henry. But Jay wasn't the owner of the outfitting business.

He'd thought about it, though. Henry was getting on in years. At some point he'd have to sell the place. Or maybe leave it to Paige to dispose of.

Jay had a few bucks in the bank from the sale of his ranch, his favorite horse and saddle. His pickup. The entire sum of his wealth.

Every day Paige must meet men at the hotel who could buy and sell the moon and the stars. All he could do was look up at them and count his blessings.

She deserved more.

By late afternoon, the rain had eased and Jay decided there was enough light left for them to make it home before dark.

Paige met his decision with a groan. The thought of getting back on Peaches and riding anywhere was the equivalent of agreeing to four hours in a dentist's chair.

She considered walking, but she didn't think she could make it. Not with her wobbly legs.

Bryan rode double with Jay, and Paige followed. As they made their way down the trail, the sun broke through the cloud cover. Slanting rays of sunshine touched the newly washed pine trees, making the needles glisten. Fir trees gave up the raindrops they'd captured, and they fell to the forest floor like tears.

Like the tears that Paige refused to shed.

When the main house finally came into view, Paige let her body go limp. Grandpa hurried off the porch to help her dismount.

"Nathan and me, we've been worried sick. When Bright Star came back without a rider—"

"I'm okay, Grandpa." She leaned on him as he helped her up onto the porch. "Bryan got thrown and twisted his ankle. Jay isn't sure how bad it is." She collapsed in one of the wicker chairs.

Jay asked Nathan to see to the horses then assisted Bryan over to the porch. The boy hopped up the steps.

Grandpa's eyes glazed with tears as he embraced the youngster. "I was afraid something awful had happened to you. Don't ever run away again, boy. It's too hard on this old man's heart."

"I'm sorry, Grandpa. I won't run away again."

He gave Paige a shy smile. "Aunt Paige says I don't have to move to Seattle. I can stay right here with you and Jay."

"Well, now, is that a fact?" Grandpa helped ease him into the chair beside Paige. She patted Bryan's arm.

Jay knelt in front of him. "Let me get that shoe off now. See how bad it is. We might have to take you to the clinic for an X-ray."

Bryan winced as his boot came off. "It feels a lot better now."

Not taking the boy's word for it, Jay checked the ankle himself. "It doesn't feel like a break, but we'll see how it is in the morning."

"Better get some ice on that swelling," Paige suggested.

"We should get out of our wet clothes." Jay stood. "Think we could all use something hot in our stomachs."

"Right, son. I'll heat up some chili." Grandpa started into the house then stopped, holding the screen door open. "One good thing happened while you were gone."

"What's that?" Paige asked.

"Archie had her puppies. She's got 'em all warm and cozy in a box in the tack room. Four of the prettiest little snub-nosed guys you'll ever see. The dad must have been a bulldog or something."

Despite her aching body, Paige's spirits lifted

and she smiled, the kind of knowing smile one woman would give to another.

A hot shower and a bowl of chili made Paige feel almost human again. While Bryan was regaling Grandpa with his now-heroic tale of frightening off a gigantic bear, Paige wandered out to the barn to visit the puppies.

The lights were still on when she found her way to the tack room. She squatted down a few feet from the cardboard box. Archie and her beautiful puppies rested on a nest of old towels. Two of the puppies had Archie's border-collie black-and-white coloring; the other two were brown with white noses.

"How are you feeling, girl?" she asked.

Archie's tail flicked up.

"Pretty proud of yourself, huh?"

One of the puppies stirred, climbed over a sibling and found a teat. Archie licked the puppy's head.

Paige inhaled a sharp, painful breath but the air didn't make it to her lungs. Oxygen couldn't slip past the blockage of regret and guilt in her chest, an obstacle so large it felt like a malignant tumor. She tried to clear her throat.

"You're going to be such a good mother," she whispered.

"You'd be a good mother, too."

Jay's voice behind her made Paige start. Before she could turn around, he hunkered down beside her.

"I'm not so sure of that," she said. "Not after the way I blew it with Bryan. I'd probably turn out to be like my mother."

He raised his brows. "And that isn't good?"

"It wasn't that Mom didn't love me and Krissy. But she and Daddy were a team. We were…an inconvenience, I think. They were both centered on what they, and the store, needed. Not what we might need or want."

"I don't think you'd be like that, Paige. Not even close."

"We'll never know, will we?" She shoved herself upright. He stood with her, his big hand on her elbow to steady her. The heat of his palm spread all the way to her diaphragm.

She drew a breath. "I'm dead on my feet. I'm going to bed."

"You'll feel better in the morning."

"I hope so." At least physically. She was less confident about her mental and emotional state.

As she walked back to the house, she glanced up at the sky. The storm had passed, leaving only a few scattered dark clouds and a sprinkling of stars.

Jay's idea of opening an Elite Hotel in Bear Lake would be laughable if she didn't half wish it were possible. A hunting and fishing lodge on the hillside above the lake designed with a long porch for sitting and window boxes of colorful flowers. A dining room with a high ceiling, paintings of royalty or maybe cowboy kings on the walls, antique tables covered in white cloths, fancy folded napkins at each place setting. Bedrooms with tall feather mattresses and canopies of silk drapes that could be pulled closed for privacy.

And tea time. Such a glorious hotel would need a fine tea service in late afternoon. People from miles around would come just to enjoy the ambience.

She laughed at the fantasy she'd conjured. But it was a bitter laugh, one that bit deep into her soul.

Dear Lord, please help me to accept the life You have given me and rejoice in Your loving goodness.

She slipped out of the house early the next morning. This would be her last day in Bear Lake for a while. She'd make the call to the courthouse to change Bryan's guardianship arrangement. Even drive up there if she had to. Then she'd head for Seattle.

For now, she wanted to revisit the place Jay had shown her, the place where both of them had felt close to God.

The natural cathedral.

He had to find a way to keep Paige in Bear Lake.

Jay knew it was a crazy thought. He'd struggled, searching for an answer all night. What could a simple wrangler and trail guide offer her?

Nothing but love and a ready-made family, *her*

family. A family he wanted to be a part of, if she'd have him.

Once up and dressed, he did his usual quick walk-through of the barn and stable to see that everything was in order.

At Peaches's stall he halted. The horse wasn't there. Thinking someone might have left the door to the corral unlatched, he stepped outside.

No Peaches.

Back in the tack room he checked for Peaches's saddle. It was gone, too.

If a thief wanted to steal a horse from Henry, Peaches would be at the bottom of the list. Any one of the string of horses he ran were worth far more.

To anyone except Paige.

He strode purposefully toward the house. Why would she want a horse? He was sure after yesterday's ordeal she'd never want to ride again.

He found Henry at the kitchen table eating a bowl of cereal.

"Where's Paige?" he asked.

Henry raised his head. "Her door was closed when I got up. I assume she's still asleep."

Jay suspected otherwise. He marched down the hall and rapped his knuckles on the door. When he didn't get a response, he quietly peeked inside.

An open suitcase sat on the neatly made bed.

His gut clenched. She was leaving this morning. There was no time left to—

"Looks like she's all packed." Henry had come up behind Jay and was peering around him.

"Yeah, it does."

"You gonna let her go, son?"

"Don't have much choice, do I?"

"Sure you do. But if you want her to stay, you gotta ask her."

"And offer her what? Being the wife of a wrangler in a town that doesn't even have a movie theater? And the biggest cultural event is a bunch of fiddle and guitar players in a country-Western festival at the municipal park."

"You'll think of something, I reckon."

Maybe. But was he ready to take the risk? The risk of loving and losing? "There's one problem. Paige is gone and so is Peaches and her saddle."

"Son, she's not planning to ride that horse all the way to Seattle. Go find her. Say what needs to be said and bring her on back here."

"Yes, sir. I'll try." He hesitated a moment thinking where Paige might have gone. In an instant he got the answer. "Wish me luck."

His nerves snapping like an electrical wire gone crazy, he jogged out to barn and saddled Thunder Boy. He'd only have one chance. He'd have to make it good.

Paige sat on a boulder listening to the roar of the waterfall cascading to the river below. The waterfall was wider and wilder this morning than when Jay had brought her here. White spray spread its reach clear to where she sat. The mist mixed with the tears on her cheeks.

The Lord's natural cathedral, Jay had called this spot.

How could she leave all this and return to Seattle? Return to a job she no longer treasured?

How could she stay here without a job?

And what could she do about her love for Jay? Although he had kissed her, and seemed to care for her, was he past the pain of losing Annie and ready to move on to someone else?

If Jay couldn't reciprocate Paige's love, it would be cruel punishment for her selfish behavior. And well deserved.

Bryan's rejection of the love and life she'd offered him was another whiplash across her conscience.

She exhaled a breath. It was time to stop being so maudlin. She wasn't a quitter. She'd follow the career she'd chosen. She'd make it a success.

She rose from the boulder, her muscles still aching from yesterday's ordeal. Untying Peaches's reins from where she had secured the horse, she started to mount.

Why not make your career a success right here in Bear Lake?

Where in the world had that thought come from?

There weren't any four-star hotels around here that hosted conferences. She had seen very little of what she'd call fine dining.

So why don't you change that? Why don't you build your own hotel?

Ha! Fat chance.

And then she remembered Elite's restored hunting lodge in England's Lake District where she'd stayed for three lovely days and nights. Bear Lake couldn't support anything quite that elegant and pricey. But a rustic lodge with lots of amenities would be doable.

Why hadn't she recognized the possibilities before?

But where on earth would she get the money to build a lodge around here? She couldn't even afford to buy the necessary land much less construct a decent building.

Pensive, she mounted Peaches and reined her back down the trail. Paige did have her condo. As small as it was, if she sold that to move here she'd have a nice chunk of money from the equity.

Maybe that would be enough money to get a bank loan and start construction on something modest.

But what about buying the land? The price of property around Bear Lake had to be enormous. This was prime recreation land with a growing year-round population.

As she reached the short trail to the overlook high above the lake, she turned off. At this early hour the lake was a clear blue sheet of glass. No wind ruffled the surface. No water-skiers cut through the stillness. The only movement on shore was a fly fisherman casting his line, drawing S-shaped patterns in the air above the water before dropping his lure on the surface to tempt a passing trout.

From this vantage point she could just make out the shape of Grandpa's wooden dock reaching out into the lake. An old rowboat rested upside down on the weathered pier.

Her thoughts skittered to a stop.

Grandpa owned some sixty or seventy acres of land, including a long stretch of lakefront property. If Grandpa would go partners with her—

A horse snorted.

She turned. Her heart lunged as she saw Jay riding toward her on Thunder Boy. Her breath tangled in her lungs as she took in the breadth of his shoulders, the length of his legs and his uncertain smile.

"I thought I'd find you at the waterfall," he said.

"I was there." The excitement of hope spun through her as he dismounted. She could be happy here with or without Jay's love. She'd have Grandpa. Hopefully, Bryan, too. Her family. "Come here. Let me show you something."

"First there's something I have to tell you before

I lose my nerve." He walked toward her and cupped her cheek with his big, callused hand. "I don't want you to leave."

Lowering his head, his lips touched hers. The warmth of his mouth on hers sent her spinning over an emotional cliff. A roar as loud as the tumbling waterfall filled her ears but it wasn't loud enough to silence her thundering heart.

"I need you to stay here with me and Bryan and Henry," he whispered against her lips.

She searched his eyes, seeking the truth. Hoping against hope that he did care about her. That she had a chance. That *they* had a chance.

"I can't offer you the world travel you've dreamed about. Or even a fancy hotel. I'm only a hired hand but I do have some money saved from selling my horse ranch. Enough so I could build us our own house—you and me and Bryan. I love you, Paige Barclay. I will love you forever, if you'll have me."

"Oh, Jay, I was so afraid—"

"I want you for my wife. The mother of my children. Fifty years from now, I want to sit on the porch holding your hand, watching the sun go down and the stars come out. I want to see you every morning with your hair mussed from sleep." He ran his fingers through her hair then brushed another kiss to her lips. "I want to kiss you every morning and every night. I want to hold you forever. Marry me. Please."

"Yes! Yes!" She wrapped her arms around his neck and kissed him with all the fierce love she felt. Love she'd feared would never be reciprocated. "I love you, Jay Red Elk. Every bit of you. I never thought I'd be content living here. But now I realize I don't have to travel the world to follow my dream. You are my dream. You and Bryan and Grandpa and Bear Lake." She took his hand and drew him to the edge of the cliff.

"We can build our life together right here." She pointed toward Grandpa's worn and weathered dock. "That hillside above the dock is a perfect place for a rustic lodge with all the amenities. Fishing, boating and horseback riding right outside the door."

He quirked his brow. "And a long porch to sit on at the end of the day."

Laughing, she hooked her arm through his. "Do you think we can do that? Pull it off? I have some equity in my condo. Bryan and Grandpa could be partners."

"Hey, don't leave me out of your dream." He turned her into his arms again. "The four of us can do anything we set our minds to. We'll create the most posh place on Bear Lake and folks will be clamoring to stay here because you'll run the best hotel in the entire West."

"I can do it. I know I can with your help."

He held her tight as they both looked out over the

lake imagining their future together. Paige sent up a prayer from her heart.

Thank You, Lord, for leading me home to Jay and the family I love.

Epilogue

The leaves on the aspen trees outside Bear Lake Community Church had begun to turn golden when Paige walked down the aisle on Grandpa's arm. Jay and Bryan waited for her at the altar, both wearing dressy jeans, cream-colored shirts and turquoise bolo ties handcrafted by Native Americans. Jay looked as nervous as Paige felt. Bryan's grin suggested he relished being in the spotlight.

Paige clung tightly to Grandpa for fear she might make a misstep. Her dress had a drop waist, handkerchief hemline and was sewn from lined lace. She wore a matching shawl around her shoulders.

Rachel Farnsworth, who Paige had been volunteering with at the thrift shop, served as her bridesmaid. She held a bouquet of bright fall flowers that matched the ones Paige carried.

The church was quite full, including Jay's warm and accepting mother and an assortment of Jay's other relatives who had come from their homes on the eastern side of the Rocky Mountains. Paige's family had suddenly multiplied many times over.

"You okay, girl?" Grandpa asked under his breath.

She forced an anxious smile. "I will be when this is over."

"You know, I wouldn't be surprised if this is what Krissy had in mind all along."

Paige stumbled and skipped a beat to stay in step with her grandfather. "Why would you say that?"

"She thought Jay would make a good catch for some girl. Think she spotted him checking you out during one of your visits."

"You mean by naming me Bryan's guardian, she was really matchmaking?"

"Could be."

Stunned by the revelation, she almost walked right into Jay, who had stepped down from the altar to greet her.

"Easy, sweetheart. No need to rush."

Grandpa handed her off to Jay, and the moment he held her hands, she knew that the family they were creating would be one filled with love and the Lord's blessing.

The ceremony led by Pastor Walker went by in a blur. Jay and Paige rode in an old Model T Ford to the reception, to be held in their own rustic hotel. During the summer they had completed the first phase of the Red Elk Lodge, including the great room with high ceilings, polished floors and rough wooden beams.

While the wedding guests admired the interior of the lodge and enjoyed the snacks prepared by Mama Machak and Nick Carbini, the chef at Pine Tree Diner, Paige only had eyes for her husband. Later they'd cut the three-tier cake provided by Love 2 Read Books and Bakery.

"Have I mentioned lately how much I love you?" she asked her groom.

"And I love you, Mrs. Red Elk. To me you will always be as beautiful as you are today."

His sweet kiss tasted of love and home.

* * * * *

Dear Reader,

I hope you've enjoyed your visit to Bear Lake, MT, and the beautiful area south of Glacier National Park. One of the treats my family enjoyed on camping vacations was horseback rides through national forest areas and national parks. Of course, in addition to the beauty of nature, I do recall a few aches and pains from using muscles not accustomed to riding a horse.

In truth I don't recall any of our trail rides led by a wrangler as handsome as Jay Red Elk. But that doesn't mean I can't fantasize such an experience. I'm glad you came along for the ride with him, too.

The death of a sister changes many lives. In this story it certainly changed the path Paige Barclay traveled in life. She learned a good deal about herself and how her family history shaped who she had become. She needed to do that before she could give and accept the love she needed.

The themes of my stories are often about creating a new family, parents and children (and even Grandpa) coming together in newly found love and appreciation for each other. I'd like to think that's not a fantasy but what can happen in real life.

I wish you all the love and happiness Paige, Jay, Bryan and Grandpa have found in their new family.

Happy reading...
Charlotte Carter

Questions for Discussion

1. Paige grew up afraid of horses; her sister Krissy loved to ride. Which sister are you more like?

2. Did you have childhood fears? How have you overcome them?

3. If you have young children, have you named the person(s), in writing, who you would want to raise them should something happen to you and your spouse? If not, why not?

4. If you work outside the home, how do you balance your work and family life?

5. Have you or any of your friends become guardians to children who have lost their parent(s)? How has that worked out? What adjustments did both adults and children need to make?

6. If you go on vacation and stay in a hotel, what services do you expect? Pool? Exercise room? Cable TV? What else?

7. Did you have dreams as a young woman to travel widely? Were you able to fulfill those dreams? If not, what stopped you?

8. If you were able to pick anywhere in the world to live, where would that be?

9. Members of the local church in this book organize receptions following a funeral service. Do the members of your church do that?

10. Churches have lots of potlucks for a variety of reasons. Are there any dishes that you avoid? Or love?

11. Do you have a favorite dish you take to potlucks? Have you shared that recipe with others?

12. Have you owned a dog that gave birth to puppies? How did the experience affect you? Or your children?

13. What did your wedding dress look like?

14. Do you or members of your family like to hunt and fish? Where is your favorite spot?

15. Do you take used clothes and other items to a thrift shop? What program(s) does the thrift shop help support?

LARGER-PRINT BOOKS!

GET 2 FREE LARGER-PRINT NOVELS PLUS 2 FREE MYSTERY GIFTS

Love Inspired®

Larger-print novels are now available...

YES! Please send me 2 FREE LARGER-PRINT Love Inspired® novels and my 2 FREE mystery gifts (gifts are worth about $10). After receiving them, if I don't wish to receive any more books, I can return the shipping statement marked "cancel." If I don't cancel, I will receive 6 brand-new novels every month and be billed just $5.24 per book in the U.S. or $5.74 per book in Canada. That's a savings of at least 23% off the cover price. It's quite a bargain! Shipping and handling is just 50¢ per book in the U.S. and 75¢ per book in Canada.* I understand that accepting the 2 free books and gifts places me under no obligation to buy anything. I can always return a shipment and cancel at any time. Even if I never buy another book, the two free books and gifts are mine to keep forever.

122/322 IDN F49Y

Name	(PLEASE PRINT)	
Address		Apt. #
City	State/Prov.	Zip/Postal Code

Signature (if under 18, a parent or guardian must sign)

Mail to the Harlequin® Reader Service:
IN U.S.A.: P.O. Box 1867, Buffalo, NY 14240-1867
IN CANADA: P.O. Box 609, Fort Erie, Ontario L2A 5X3

**Are you a current subscriber to Love Inspired books and want to receive the larger-print edition?
Call 1-800-873-8635 or visit www.ReaderService.com.**

* Terms and prices subject to change without notice. Prices do not include applicable taxes. Sales tax applicable in N.Y. Canadian residents will be charged applicable taxes. Offer not valid in Quebec. This offer is limited to one order per household. Not valid for current subscribers to Love Inspired Larger-Print books. All orders subject to credit approval. Credit or debit balances in a customer's account(s) may be offset by any other outstanding balance owed by or to the customer. Please allow 4 to 6 weeks for delivery. Offer available while quantities last.

Your Privacy—The Harlequin® Reader Service is committed to protecting your privacy. Our Privacy Policy is available online at www.ReaderService.com or upon request from the Harlequin Reader Service.

We make a portion of our mailing list available to reputable third parties that offer products we believe may interest you. If you prefer that we not exchange your name with third parties, or if you wish to clarify or modify your communication preferences, please visit us at www.ReaderService.com/consumerschoice or write to us at Harlequin Reader Service Preference Service, P.O. Box 9062, Buffalo, NY 14269. Include your complete name and address.

LILPDIR13R

LARGER-PRINT BOOKS!

GET 2 FREE LARGER-PRINT NOVELS PLUS 2 FREE MYSTERY GIFTS

Love Inspired®
SUSPENSE
RIVETING INSPIRATIONAL ROMANCE

Larger-print novels are now available...

YES! Please send me 2 FREE LARGER-PRINT Love Inspired® Suspense novels and my 2 FREE mystery gifts (gifts are worth about $10). After receiving them, if I don't wish to receive any more books, I can return the shipping statement marked "cancel." If I don't cancel, I will receive 4 brand-new novels every month and be billed just $5.24 per book in the U.S. or $5.74 per book in Canada. That's a savings of at least 23% off the cover price. It's quite a bargain! Shipping and handling is just 50¢ per book in the U.S. and 75¢ per book in Canada.* I understand that accepting the 2 free books and gifts places me under no obligation to buy anything. I can always return a shipment and cancel at any time. Even if I never buy another book, the two free books and gifts are mine to keep forever.

110/310 IDN F5CC

Name	(PLEASE PRINT)
Address	Apt. #
City	State/Prov.	Zip/Postal Code

Signature (if under 18, a parent or guardian must sign)

Mail to the **Harlequin® Reader Service:**
IN U.S.A.: P.O. Box 1867, Buffalo, NY 14240-1867
IN CANADA: P.O. Box 609, Fort Erie, Ontario L2A 5X3

Are you a current subscriber to Love Inspired Suspense books and want to receive the larger-print edition?
Call 1-800-873-8635 or visit www.ReaderService.com.

* Terms and prices subject to change without notice. Prices do not include applicable taxes. Sales tax applicable in N.Y. Canadian residents will be charged applicable taxes. Offer not valid in Quebec. This offer is limited to one order per household. Not valid for current subscribers to Love Inspired Suspense larger-print books. All orders subject to credit approval. Credit or debit balances in a customer's account(s) may be offset by any other outstanding balance owed by or to the customer. Please allow 4 to 6 weeks for delivery. Offer available while quantities last.

Your Privacy—The Harlequin® Reader Service is committed to protecting your privacy. Our Privacy Policy is available online at www.ReaderService.com or upon request from the Harlequin Reader Service.

We make a portion of our mailing list available to reputable third parties that offer products we believe may interest you. If you prefer that we not exchange your name with third parties, or if you wish to clarify or modify your communication preferences, please visit us at www.ReaderService.com/consumerchoice or write to us at Harlequin Reader Service Preference Service, P.O. Box 9062, Buffalo, NY 14269. Include your complete name and address.

LISLPDIR13R

REQUEST YOUR FREE BOOKS!
2 FREE WHOLESOME ROMANCE NOVELS
IN LARGER PRINT
PLUS 2
FREE
MYSTERY GIFTS

HEARTWARMING™

Wholesome, tender romances

YES! Please send me 2 FREE Harlequin® Heartwarming Larger-Print novels and my 2 FREE mystery gifts (gifts worth about $10). After receiving them, if I don't wish to receive any more books, I can return the shipping statement marked "cancel." If I don't cancel, I will receive 4 brand-new larger-print novels every month and be billed just $4.99 per book in the U.S. or $5.74 per book in Canada. That's a savings of at least 23% off the cover price. It's quite a bargain! Shipping and handling is just 50¢ per book in the U.S. and 75¢ per book in Canada.* I understand that accepting the 2 free books and gifts places me under no obligation to buy anything. I can always return a shipment and cancel at any time. Even if I never buy another book, the two free books and gifts are mine to keep forever.

161/361 IDN F47N

Name	(PLEASE PRINT)	

Address		Apt. #

City	State/Prov.	Zip/Postal Code

Signature (if under 18, a parent or guardian must sign)

Mail to the **Harlequin® Reader Service:**
IN U.S.A.: P.O. Box 1867, Buffalo, NY 14240-1867
IN CANADA: P.O. Box 609, Fort Erie, Ontario L2A 5X3

* Terms and prices subject to change without notice. Prices do not include applicable taxes. Sales tax applicable in N.Y. Canadian residents will be charged applicable taxes. Offer not valid in Quebec. This offer is limited to one order per household. Not valid for current subscribers to Harlequin Heartwarming larger-print books. All orders subject to credit approval. Credit or debit balances in a customer's account(s) may be offset by any other outstanding balance owed by or to the customer. Please allow 4 to 6 weeks for delivery. Offer available while quantities last.

Your Privacy—The Harlequin® Reader Service is committed to protecting your privacy. Our Privacy Policy is available online at www.ReaderService.com or upon request from the Harlequin Reader Service.

We make a portion of our mailing list available to reputable third parties that offer products we believe may interest you. If you prefer that we not exchange your name with third parties, or if you wish to clarify or modify your communication preferences, please visit us at www.ReaderService.com/consumerchoice or write to us at Harlequin Reader Service Preference Service, P.O. Box 9062, Buffalo, NY 14269. Include your complete name and address.

HWDIR13R

Reader Service.com

Manage your account online!

- Review your order history
- Manage your payments
- Update your address

---

*We've designed
the Harlequin® Reader Service
website just for you.*

Enjoy all the features!

- Reader excerpts from any series
- Respond to mailings and
  special monthly offers
- Discover new series available to you
- Browse the Bonus Bucks catalog
- Share your feedback

Visit us at:
ReaderService.com